"Is there something I can do for you?"

Jethro then made a minor production out of looking at his watch, as if counting the seconds he could spare her.

Allie made a huge effort to drag herself together. She squared her shoulders, sucked some air into her cramped lungs and managed to say coolly, "I need a favor, and I'm willing to pay handsomely for it."

The only response to that was the slight upward drift of one sable brow. It incensed her.

"If you're not interested, then please say so, and I won't waste any more of your valuable time!"

"I'm curious to know what favor you're willing to pay so highly for."

"I need you to marry me," she said.

DIANA HAMILTON is a true romantic and fell in love with her husband at first sight. They still live in the fairy-tale Tudor house in England where they raised their three children. Now the idyll is shared with eight rescued cats and a puppy. But despite an often chaotic lifestyle, ever since she learned to read and write Diana has had her nose in a book—either reading or writing one—and plans to go on doing just that for a very long time to come.

Books by Diana Hamilton

HARLEQUIN PRESENTS®
2072—THE FAITHFUL WIFE
2094—MISTRESS FOR A NIGHT

Don't miss any of our special offers. Write to us at the following address for information on our newest releases.

Harlequin Reader Service
U.S.: 3010 Walden Ave., P.O. Box 1325, Buffalo, NY 14269
Canadian: P.O. Box 609, Fort Erie, Ont. L2A 5X3

Diana Hamilton

BOUGHT: ONE HUSBAND

TORONTO • NEW YORK • LONDON
AMSTERDAM • PARIS • SYDNEY • HAMBURG
STOCKHOLM • ATHENS • TOKYO • MILAN • MADRID
PRAGUE • WARSAW • BUDAPEST • AUCKLAND

ISBN 0-373-12132-6

BOUGHT: ONE HUSBAND

First North American Publication 2000.

Copyright © 1999 by Diana Hamilton.

CHAPTER ONE

JETHRO COLE secured the aluminium extending ladder on the roof rack and stowed the bucket and window leathers in the back of the old van. Then he wiped the sweat from his brow with a tanned forearm and pushed the unruly fall of black hair out of the way with impatient fingers. Past time he got a haircut.

He expelled a slow, relaxing breath through even white teeth. The end of another long working day, clambering up and down ladders in the hot July sun, cleaning other people's windows. At least he was beginning to get the hang of it now, and not collecting too many complaints about smears and missed corners.

He had collected a couple of propositions from bored housewives, though, which he had pretended not to understand in order to avoid giving offence and to keep their custom, and now he was getting loud and appreciative wolf whistles, by the sound of it!

Digging into the pockets of his battered jeans for the ignition key, he watched with barely concealed amusement as the perpetrators drew level. A brace of teenaged girls, arm in arm, with wildly permed hair, identical pairs of fake leather jeans and skimpy tops that left nothing whatsoever to the imagination.

'You can peer through my windows any time, gorgeous!' said the one with the nose-stud, while the other simply giggled through a mouthful of gum as they teetered away on mile-high heels in the direction of the High Street, obviously in search of whatever Shrewsbury offered in the way of night-life.

His self-inflicted lurch into the one-man window-cleaning business was showing him a slice of life never glimpsed in the sophisticated, air-conditioned, superficially polite world of mega-big financial wheeling and dealing, and his grin was rakish, his amber eyes glinting with humour as he slid behind the wheel and coaxed the reluctant engine into spluttering life.

He was driving around in a beat-up old van while his Jaguar XK8 convertible was gathering dust in a lock-up on the other side of town, wearing scuffed jeans and a faded T-shirt that should have been binned years ago while his designer casuals were folded away in a suitcase back at 182 Albert Terrace.

He'd stayed there a whole lot longer than he'd originally intended. In normal circumstances an overnight stop to catch up with his former nanny's news was as long as it got.

But here he still was, cleaning windows instead of directing operations and steering his varied enterprises from one or other of his worldwide boardrooms. Or unwinding in his isolated cottage for a couple of weeks, as had been his intention.

Because when he'd stopped off to pay his respects to Nanny Briggs, as he always did *en route* to his country home—roughly every twelve months—his schedule had been turned on its head.

And, despite his original grit-your-teeth-and-get-on-with-it attitude, he was enjoying every minute! And he would, he reminded himself drily, be enjoying it a whole lot more if he were getting what he wanted, or at least getting close to it.

He was experiencing the type of excitement that usually came when he was close to finalising a fantastic deal, and which never before in his thirty-four years of living had been associated with a woman.

Women came easily.

But not this one. Not Alissa Brannan.

His pursuit of her delectable person wasn't making much progress, he had to admit, but he'd get there. He always got what he wanted, didn't he?

He wouldn't have built up a massive business empire, practically from scratch, if he'd allowed failure a look-in, he reminded himself. Besides, pursuing a woman carried a rare excitement for a man who'd been relentlessly hunted since he was in his early twenties and notching up his second million.

His mood was reflective as he drew out into traffic. He had first seen Alissa Brannan around a year ago. She'd been performing on the catwalk at a showing of a talented Italian designer's first collection, and he, Jethro, a connoisseur of beautiful women, had been impressed. Very impressed.

If he hadn't been accompanying his woman of the moment he might have done something about it. But while his occasional affairs lasted he was loyal; it was part of his unwritten code.

That very evening, he remembered, that particular relationship had ended, with the customary gift of a piece of expensive jewellery and no recriminations on either side. Another part of the unwritten code.

Discreet enquiries had given him the information that Alissa Brannan, the exciting new clotheshorse all the top designers were suddenly frantic for, had the reputation of a recluse. Apparently she never dated and socialised rarely—charity functions were about the size of it.

He'd be the one to make her change her mind about dating. That was the promise he'd made himself. But he hadn't been able to do a thing about it because his work had taken him overseas and kept him there for long stretches of time.

Any other woman, briefly fancied, would have quickly faded from his mind, forever forgotten in the larger importance of empire-building. But somehow those exquisitely lovely features, the grace of her willowy body, had stuck in his mind.

There hadn't been another woman in the last twelve months, despite the offers. He'd told himself he was too busy jetting around the world from one boardroom to the other, that at the age of thirty-four his appetites were slowing down.

But meeting her again, in the backstreets of this quaint old medieval town, had told him that there was no danger of him slowing down—not in that department!

He negotiated a busy roundabout and took the exit that would lead him to the downmarket side of town, his mind totally occupied with thoughts of the beautiful, elusive creature who had somehow got right under his skin.

Meeting her had turned what had been a week of doing his duty by Nanny Briggs and her husband Harry into something else entirely. It had been too much of a coincidence to be anything other than fate.

He caught the thought and tossed it around. Fate? He didn't believe in it. He was in control of his own destiny. He took life by the scruff of the neck and shook it until it fell into his preferred pattern.

So why was Alissa giving him the cold shoulder?

His black brows were pulled into a frown as he parked the van in front of 182 Albert Terrace. He swung his long legs out, slammed the door behind him and strode across the blistering pavement, his bleak mood dissipating when he discovered Nanny Briggs behind the dusty hedge, watering the pots of geraniums that brightened the narrow strip of front garden.

'Good news, Master Jethro—Harry's back on his feet again and ready for work.' She smiled up at him, and at six-two he towered over her short, round person. To her he would always be Master Jethro, even when he was ninety. 'And we can't thank you enough for taking over. Harry was so worried. He was sure his clients would go elsewhere, the business being so new.'

It was barely six months old, started when the older

man had been made redundant from the local factory. Harry had no intention of living off the state, not while he could work. Harry had his pride.

'I was only too happy to do it, you know that.' He watched as she watered the last of the pots. A week ago that hadn't been true. He'd do anything for Nanny Briggs, but that didn't mean that spending a week cleaning windows could be viewed as anything other than a pain. But he'd done what he'd seen as his duty, and duty obviously had its own rewards because he'd met Alissa again—or Allie, as he'd learned she preferred to be called.

'You'll be ready for a cup of tea. Wash your hands in the scullery while I make it.' She headed into the house and Jethro followed. 'Harry's having his bath now. You can have yours before supper. I've made a shepherd's pie. It always was one of your favourites.'

Jethro went to do as he was told. Some things would never change, and the dishing up of nursery food was one of them! But he grinned as he scrubbed up in the scullery, listening to the comforting rattle of china coming from the small but scrupulously clean kitchen.

She'd married Harry Ford when they were both in their fifties, but to him she would always be Nanny Briggs, the linchpin of his early years. The only mothering he'd ever had had come from her, his own mother having been too interested in enjoying herself to be bothered with either him or his younger sister Chloe.

He rubbed the moisture from his hands and face on

a scratchy towel—Nanny Briggs didn't believe in pampering—and walked back into the kitchen smelling of strong carbolic soap.

'Drink your tea before it gets cold and tell me what your plans are,' she invited. 'I feel guilty enough as it is about breaking into your holiday, so I don't want to hear you're heading back to London, or Amsterdam or wherever. You work too hard.'

He pulled a chair out from the square scrubbed pine table and sat, long legs stretched out in front of him, smiling because she looked so stern. Then the smile faded because she looked something else, he thought with a pang: tired, careworn, more elderly than middle-aged.

His plans? Harry's welcome recovery from a bout of summer flu left him free to go on his way, to get on with his life and to take that well-earned break at his cottage on the Shropshire/Welsh border, if he still wanted to.

He didn't think he'd bother, because Harry's recovery also left him free to step up his pursuit of the seemingly unwilling Allie. Unwittingly, he glowered at his empty cup. He also needed to do something more for Nanny Briggs and Harry. He had always thought of Nanny Briggs as being indestructible, but she wasn't. It was time she started to take life more easily, and spent her remaining years free of financial worry.

'I thought I might stay on with you for another couple of days, if that's OK with you.' He watched her closely as she reached for his empty cup and refilled it. 'There's a business proposition I'd like to put to Harry.' And he'd figure out a way so it wouldn't smell of charity.

Allie paid off the cab and stood on the pavement, staring up at her apartment block in a daze. She, who despised liars, had just told the biggest whopper in the history of the world!

Despite the cloud cover that blanketed London her skin felt as if it were on fire, perspiration beading her short upper lip, all her bones wobbling. She didn't know how she was going to make it into the building.

But she managed it somehow, feeling distinctly queasy as the lift whisked her up to her floor, and practically hysterical when it took her a good two minutes to fit her key into the lock.

Which served her right for telling the solicitor such a barefaced lie!

Tottering into her small, minimally furnished sitting room, she told herself to calm down, and fast. She had very little time to turn the lie into truth, and getting hysterical was wasting it.

Walking out of her high-heeled pumps, she headed for the bedroom, releasing her shimmering blonde hair from the pins that had held it in a sophisticated coil at the nape of her long, elegant neck.

Out of the classy suit she'd worn for the meeting, she pulled on a pair of old blue jeans and a baggy T-shirt. Now she felt more like herself and less like a super-model, and that helped the calming down process.

Cleaning off her make-up, she reviewed the situation objectively, recalling her initial mild curiosity when she'd complied with her late uncle's solicitor's request for a meeting.

'Perhaps he left you something in his will?' Laura, her mother, had suggested. She never said her brother-in-law's name; 'Fabian' was a word that hadn't crossed her lips since what had happened several years ago. 'Maybe towards the end he felt guilty.' Her voice hadn't carried much conviction.

'Pigs might fly!' Allie had smiled into her mother's deep blue eyes, so like her own. 'Knowing him, he's probably left me a shovel to dig my grave with!'

So, only mildly curious, she'd broken into the long summer break she'd given herself in order to spend time with Laura, whose deepening depression was worrying her, combining the meeting with Uncle Fabian's solicitor with an overnight stay at her modest London apartment and a working dinner with her agent.

Leaving the cramped terraced house on the outskirts of Shrewsbury, which Laura now shared with her sister Fran, Allie had caught the connecting train to Euston and spent the journey doing sums in her head.

A year ago she'd been on the point of giving up a modelling career that had seemed to be going nowhere when she'd suddenly hit the big time. Since that day she'd been saving hard, and now she had enough to put a hefty deposit on a home in the country for Laura and Fran to share.

Close enough to town for Fran to commute to her job in the council offices, with a large enough garden for Laura to indulge the passion for plants that had developed during the years they'd spent at Studley, when she'd transformed the neglected gardens into paradise. Her mother would never be remotely happy living in town; she needed open spaces and birdsong.

So, providing the high-paying assignments continued to come her way—and at just twenty-two she still had a few good years ahead of her—she could take on a mortgage and make her mother a generous allowance. She hated having to see her taking on any cleaning work she could get just to pay her way.

Which was why she'd taken this break from international catwalks and photographic studios. Apart from recouping her energies after a year of unremitting hard work, she knew she would need time to persuade her mother to accept the money. Only last night, after Fran had gone to bed, she'd broached the subject.

'I refuse to let you spend your money on me. It's sweet of you, darling, but I can't let you do it.' Laura's eyes had misted with the tears that now never seemed far away, but Allie had insisted.

'The money wouldn't be wasted; property's a good investment. And as for the allowance—what else have I got to spend my money on?'

Apart from the rental on her small flat, and a few decent clothes for public appearances, she needed very little. Unlike most of her colleagues, she rarely socialised, and wasn't interested in expensive holidays or status symbol cars.

She'd pressed her point home. 'I only decided to go for a modelling career to earn money fast, so that I could do this for you. For years I thought the big bucks wouldn't come, but now they have I don't expect you to go all mulish on me! I know how happy you were at Studley, and that even after Dad died you'd have gone back like a shot had it been possible. I can't give you Studley back—I wish I could—but I can give you a country cottage. It will be up to you to put the roses round the door!'

As soon as she'd seen her mother's mouth begin to quiver she regretted having mentioned Studley. Laura had been devoted to the place. Still was. All her happy memories were there.

So, Allie's mind had been occupied with worrying about the way her mother seemed to be going downhill, with racking her brains for the right tack to take to persuade her to accept what Allie could offer her, right up until the moment when the solicitor had seen her seated and told her, 'Your late uncle, Fabian Brannan left his entire estate to the nation. Apart from the property known as Studley Manor, and its contents, which goes to you.'

He glanced at her, pushing his glasses back onto the bridge of his nose. 'There is, however, one condition.' He raised one eyebrow and permitted himself an almost imperceptible shrug. 'That you are married at the time of his death, or within one month of it.'

Allie stared into his bland brown eyes, stunned. Her stomach churned sickeningly. She wanted to scream.

Her initial reaction to the first part of his statement had been a huge upsurge of elation. Fabian, at the end, had made amends. Studley Manor, the lovely old house where she'd spent the first fifteen years of her life, the place where her mother yearned to be, where her most treasured memories were, was within her gift.

Laura would be happy there, after years of drudgery. She would have her memories of better times, would be at last content, finding peace working in the beautiful gardens she had created out of a virtual wilderness.

But the condition Fabian had imposed took it all away from her. He had known, because she had once told him in no uncertain terms, that she would never marry, never entrust her happiness and security to a mere man.

The condition he had made was nothing but an elderly man's spite, the vicious sting in the tail.

Just for one moment she knew what real, gut-twisting hatred was. Then she made herself breathe, expelled the frozen air from her lungs, and told herself that Fabian wouldn't get the last laugh because she wouldn't let him. Brazenly, she lied.

'I don't see a problem there. My fiancé and I didn't intend to marry until the end of the year. But there's no reason why we shouldn't bring the date forward to comply with that condition.'

She gave him a cool, level look down the length

of her neat nose, saw his eyes flick down to her ring-less fingers and calmly told another whopper. 'I don't wear my ring on a day-to-day basis; it's far too valu-able. I'd be afraid of losing it, or getting mugged.' She got to her feet, smoothing non-existent creases from her skirt, collecting her bag. 'We have a month, you say?'

'Actually, rather less.' He rose when she did, glanc-ing down at the document on his desk. 'Your uncle died a week ago, as you know. There are three weeks left—a day or two over if we take it as a calendar month. I did try to persuade him against making that condition, but to no avail.'

'Fabian was a stubborn man,' she agreed. And she left, the stupidity of what she'd done hitting her as soon as she reached the street.

That lie had been instinctive, she thought now. A need to hold onto the dream of giving Studley back to her mother.

She, too, had wonderful memories of the years when she and her parents had lived at Studley, but she should have walked out of that office the moment that condition had been mentioned, dismissing it for the evil taunt it was.

But her mother still wanted to go back, and it would be smooth, poetic justice if she could take the legacy he'd so briefly dangled under her nose, then snatched away with that hateful condition of his.

But how? How could she hope to turn that lie into the truth?

She went through to the kitchen and made herself

a strong black coffee. She leant against the work surface, sipping it, frowning.

Many men had tried to date her in the past, but she hadn't been interested—too wary of so-called commitment to fall into that trap. She wasn't into casual sex, and she had no intention of getting into a serious relationship, so what was the point?

She wasn't vain about the looks she'd inherited from her mother, simply regarding them as an asset— like a good head for business or a talent for interior design—and using them accordingly, working hard to give her mother back some of the happiness she had lost.

Surely she could use those looks to get herself a husband?

She put her mug down and began to pace the shoe-box-sized room her eyes half closed in concentration. There had to be a way. She could put on her glad rags and go out partying, pick out an unattached male and—

Allie stopped herself right there. She wasn't a complete idiot, so why was she thinking like one?

No sane man would agree to marry in an almighty hurry—and in name only; that went without saying— just so she could claim her inheritance, then disappear as soon as the deeds were safely lodged with her, and file for divorce a couple of years later!

No sex, no strings. Nothing in it for him. No man would go for that. She had very little time and nothing to offer in the way of inducement, except— She stopped pacing, her eyes going wide as the answer hit her.

Except money!

She could *buy* herself a short-term husband!

There was the more than healthy sum she'd hoarded with the intention of settling her mother and Fran in a country cottage. If Studley was hers, she wouldn't need it.

And she knew just the man who might accept her proposition.

He'd be more than presentable once he was tidied up—with the type of looks that would send most women dreamy-eyed. So people wouldn't be totally amazed if she married him, and that solicitor wouldn't suspect there was something fishy going on.

She'd have to take a chance on his trustworthiness, but she already knew that he had a kind and caring disposition. And he was poverty-struck, or as good as. Surely he would jump at the opportunity of earning himself a nice little nest-egg.

True, she'd been introduced to him barely a week ago, and, true again, he'd made his interest in her more than plain. But she'd fended him off, coolly and politely, with the ease of long practice. So she'd have to make it perfectly clear that there would be no hanky-panky.

She could handle that. Of course she could. No worries there.

Crossing the room, she picked up the phone and cancelled dinner with her agent, then walked determinedly to the bedroom and began to pack.

Jethro Cole, the rookie window-cleaner, was her only hope.

CHAPTER TWO

'I CAN only suppose,' said Nanny Briggs as she carried the coffee tray through to the sitting room, 'that since Harry swallowed that pride of his and accepted you as a partner, your staying on here has something to do with that very pretty young woman who stopped by last week to thank you for picking her mother up off the pavement.'

Jethro folded the *FT* with an impatient crackle. He didn't know why the hell he was still here, making a damn fool of himself. And he most certainly didn't want to discuss it.

He glared moodily back over the last eight days: to his first day here, on what had been supposedly a flying visit, to find Harry—judging by the sound of his moans and groans—lying on his deathbed, in a fret because he was letting his customers down and his van was in to get the clutch fixed, so how could he get it, the state he was in, and how could he climb ladders when he could barely stand?

Nanny Briggs had never learned to drive, so Jethro had collected the pile of rust from a garage a few streets away. Driving back, a slender, neatly dressed woman had collapsed on the pavement. Alissa's mother, as he'd discovered later.

When she'd recovered sufficiently to tell him she'd

never fainted in her life before he'd driven her home, insisted on making her some tea, and stayed with her until her sister returned from work.

The woman, Laura Brannan—and even then he hadn't made the connection—had once been very lovely, but her frailty, her pallor, the sadness in her eyes, had worried him. On his way out he'd taken her sister aside. 'I don't want to sound alarmist, but I think you should persuade her to get a check-up.'

'I can try. But she won't take time off. If she'd trained for a proper career, instead of relying on some useless man, then she wouldn't have to go out cleaning other people's houses all day and offices half the night. And she wouldn't get herself worn ragged.'

Sister Fran was a man-hater, obviously. He'd said goodbye and put the incident out of his mind. But the next day, up a ladder, washing Nanny Briggs' windows because Harry, though grateful for his offer to hold the fort had refused to let him loose on his customers until he'd seen what kind of a pig's ear he made of the job, the woman who'd lingered in his mind for twelve months had stopped to thank him for coming to her mother's aid.

Seeing her again had sent him into a tailspin, made him speechless, but as soon as he'd got his head together he'd made up his mind. This time she wouldn't get away. This time he wouldn't be too busy to make the follow-up.

That evening, for some reason he hadn't worked out at the time, he'd put on old but clean jeans, topped by a faded T-shirt—the sort of rough and ready gear he wore around his country home while knocking in fenceposts or helping the full-time gardener—and walked the short distance to where he now knew she was staying with her mother, carrying a bunch of flowers. For Laura.

And he had earned himself an hour of tea and chat.

Laura's pleasure in the flowers, her touching gratitude that he had remembered where she lived, had stung his conscience—particularly when it had become obvious that she thought he was a window-cleaner, struggling to make a living.

During that hour he had learned a couple of things: Alissa—or Allie, as she preferred to be called—would be staying in the area for a few weeks. And she didn't want him to know how she earned her living because she had killed the conversation stone-dead when Laura had begun to say something about a fashion shoot.

It was as if she didn't want him to imagine the glamorous side of her life, to look at her with male speculation. But, if she had but known it, he'd found her even more loin-stirringly desirable in the inexpensive cotton skirt and sleeveless top she'd been wearing.

The soft fabric had swayed against her lissom body as she'd walked, hinting at the tender curve of her breasts, the long and elegant line of her thighs. The feminine grace of her had brought a lump to his throat; he didn't think he'd seen anything as beautiful as the way she moved.

And he hadn't been able to tear his eyes away from

the delicacy of her bone structure in repose: the long, heavily lashed and fascinating deep blue eyes, the sensual curve of her unpainted mouth. Just looking at her had given him problems with certain parts of his anatomy, but he hadn't been able to tear his eyes away.

He had also earned himself an invitation to supper the following evening. Though he'd seen the quick frown Allie had given her mother, her bored smile when he'd accepted. It hadn't squashed him. He loved nothing better than a challenge. A challenge of any kind made the adrenalin flow. And he had walked back to 182 vowing complacently that before she knew what had hit her he'd be kissing the boredom from those sultry lips.

'Do I take it, from your grumpy expression, that you haven't got any further than taking tea with her mother?' Nanny Briggs handed him his coffee, black and strong, just the way he liked it. He shook his head at the plate of biscuits she pushed over the low table towards him and wished she'd drop the subject.

He ground his teeth when she didn't. 'Most evenings last week you popped out "to see how Mrs Brannan's getting on" and came back with that grim, determined look on your face. You can't argue with that!'

He wasn't. He'd taken up Laura's invitation to supper with alacrity, sure he'd make progress in his pursuit of Allie. He'd done no such thing. On subsequent evenings when he'd 'just dropped by' his hopefully casual-seeming suggestions that Allie might join him in a walk by the river, a stroll downtown to pick up a Chinese takeaway, had been politely but firmly turned down.

Her rejection had only fuelled his determination to change her mind, make her as hot for him as he was for her. Until last night.

Last night Laura had informed him that Allie was back in London, and in her gentle, roundabout way had told him that she was sorry, really sorry, but he was wasting his time. Her daughter wasn't interested in men.

The implication had been plain.

Alissa Brannan was gay.

He had stumped back through the twilit streets blisteringly angry—more with himself for being such a twit than with Allie herself—and railroaded Harry into accepting him as a sleeping partner and a fat injection of cash.

'Expansion's the name of the game. Buy a respectable, reliable van, get your name and phone number on the sides, take on a school-leaver and train him up—a mere half of the enquiries I had to turn down last week because there simply wasn't the time to fit them in would pay a lad's wages. You'll never do more than just scrape by if you don't.'

His accountant would swing things so that the inflow of capital into Harry's business didn't dry up, and ensure that the elderly man never discovered that the money came out of Jethro's own personal account. Nanny Briggs' future would be more secure.

That taken care of, and today Harry out inspecting

the good-as-new van he'd seen on the forecourt when he'd taken his old one in for a clutch job, he was trying to rake up the energy and enthusiasm to take that deferred break, pack his bags and clear out.

And forget Alissa Brannan.

But Nanny Briggs had other ideas. She told him tartly, 'You should tidy yourself up, Master Jethro. Wear something decent when you go calling. Take her some flowers and a nice box of chocolates.'

Nanny telling him how to woo a lady was beyond bearing, and short of telling her to put a sock in it, that up until now he'd had no trouble getting women into his bed, and more than a little keeping them out of it, there seemed to be no stopping her.

He'd have bought Allie a chocolate factory and a field full of flowers. He would have given her the moon! But, misguided sucker that he was, he'd stuck to the fiction of struggling to make a living. His self-admittedly cynical view of women had told him that his millions would make his pursuit, and her capitulation, a damn sight easier. But, blind fool that he was, he hadn't wanted that. He'd wanted her to want him for himself, not for his wealth.

That had been before he'd learned that she was gay. He felt like the world's biggest fool.

He swallowed the last of his coffee and snapped to his feet. He was out of here! Nanny, looking as if butter wouldn't melt in her mouth, was fussing around the room, tweaking the net window drapes back into place, doubtlessly thinking up another snippet of advice on how to arrange his love life.

He was about to announce his intention to collect his Jag, head for the hills, when Nanny's voice rooted him to the spot. 'Your pursuit doesn't appear to be as one-sided as we thought it was. The young lady you're interested in is about to ring the doorbell.'

Allie had never felt this strung up before in her entire life. Ever since she'd turned the corner and seen Jethro's old van parked outside 182 she'd been pacing up and down, trying to find the courage to face him.

She'd meant to make it easy on herself, leave a message with his grandmother, ask him to call round after he'd finished work because she had a favour to ask him.

Some favour!

She knew he lived with his grandmother because she remembered asking him, over supper that night, if he lived locally. He'd said, 'At the moment I'm staying with Nan—' biting off the word, as if he were ashamed of having to live with a relative at his age, not being able to afford a place of his own.

And she knew where his gran lived because that day when Allie had been driving her mother to the local supermarket in Fran's car, Laura had put a hand on her arm and urged, 'Do stop, Allie. There's that nice young man who took me home after I fainted in the street. I know I didn't thank him properly, and I'd like to do it now.'

The little white-haired old lady who'd been standing at the foot of the ladder, issuing instructions, telling him to get right into the corners, had glowed with pride when Laura had explained what had happened and called her thanks up the ladder. Allie had added hers, because anyone who was kind to her mother got her vote, and the man on the receiving end had looked as if he'd gone into shock. It had been left to the old lady to agree that her Jethro had his heart in the right place, had been brought up to know what was what. They must excuse him for not coming down the ladder, she'd said, because he was new to the window-cleaning business, but a very quick learner.

Allie had switched off at that point. Jethro had appeared unable to say a word for himself. He was obviously painfully shy, and probably not very bright. She had felt deeply sorry for him.

There he'd been—in his early thirties, she guessed...up a ladder trying to learn how to be a window-cleaner when with his looks, that soft near-black hair, that deeply attractive, very masculine face, that perfect physique, he could earn himself a fortune as a male model.

Gently she'd urged her mother away, to spare him any further embarrassment.

Her opinions had done an abrupt turnaround when he'd called by with a huge bunch of flowers for her mother, relaxed and extremely self-assured. Every time he'd looked at her he'd eaten her with his eyes, and each time he'd tried to date her she'd turned him down, and hoped he'd got the message that she wasn't interested in what he had in mind.

And now she was going to have to ask him to marry her!

Her stomach lurched and began to ache. She wrapped her arms about her middle for comfort and tried to stand confidently at his front door.

It would have been so much easier to leave a message. That would have given her loads more time to get herself together, work out what to say and how to say it. So why wasn't he out on his rounds?

Too lazy to get out of bed? Lost all his customers through incompetence? Or perhaps that awful old van had finally died.

Whatever, he'd leap at the opportunity of earning himself a lump of cash. Wouldn't he?

She really had no option but to ask. She'd arrived back in Shrewsbury late last night, but not late enough, because Laura had still been up, watching an old movie on TV, so she'd had to explain what had been said when she'd visited Fabian's solicitor. 'Word for word,' her mother had demanded.

She hadn't wanted to mention it until she'd got it sorted, or given up on the project. But she couldn't lie to her mother; she could only lie to solicitors!

The look of stunned happiness on the older woman's face when she'd heard that her late brother-in-law had left Studley Manor to her daughter had pained Allie even more than the resigned defeat in the blue eyes when she'd explained about the condition.

'That's that, then,' Laura had sighed. 'He always had a cruel streak.'

Allie had hugged her, more determined than ever to get her mother what she wanted: the lovely home

she'd been pining for all these years. 'Don't say anything to anyone, and don't be surprised by anything
that happens. I think I know a way to get Studley
back.'

Easy enough to say when in the grip of powerful
emotions, but a different thing entirely in the cold
light of day.

She had no option but to try. He could only say
no. Straightening her body, she tucked a tendril of
hair that had escaped from her no-nonsense ponytail
behind her ear.

The door opened almost before she'd taken her finger from the bell, and his grandmother said, 'It's Miss
Brannan, isn't it? Do come in.'

There was something very reassuring about the
starchiness of the white apron that covered the plump
body, the stern expression on the lined face which
was belied by twinkling eyes. His grandmother was
someone a girl could rely on, Allie thought, clutching
at straws, buying extra time, and gabbled, 'I don't
want to intrude. Perhaps you could give Jethro a message for me?'

'Why not give it to him yourself?' She stood aside,
defying Allie to do anything other.

Trying to stamp down on the million butterflies that
had been let loose in her stomach, Allie crossed the
threshold because she had no choice. The old lady
plainly had no time for ditherers, and could, she
guessed from the firm set of her mouth, become quite
alarming when crossed.

'Through here.' A door leading off the minuscule

hallway was pushed open decisively. 'Speak your mind and put the poor boy out of his misery one way or another. No shilly-shallying.'

A firm hand propelled her into a small living room furnished with ponderous Victorian pieces. She heard the door close behind her and found herself staring at Jethro Cole's broad-shouldered back.

He appeared to be engrossed in the view from the window, but what he could actually see through the thick net drapes she couldn't imagine. And what on earth his grandmother had meant by putting him out of his misery was beyond her. And if she tried to puzzle it out she would get even more flustered than she already was.

Her heart thumping, she tentatively cleared her throat and watched him very slowly turn to face her. It was, she thought sinkingly, like looking at a stranger. Gone was the casually charming sexy male with the hazy golden eyes that had always seemed to be stripping her naked, and in his place was a man whose features had hardened into something approaching arrogance, whose eyes held a cold yellow indifference.

Dressed, as usual, in old jeans, faded T-shirt and beat-up trainers, he managed to wear an aura of power, of control. He was, she realised, her eyes widening, far more alarming than his indomitable grandmother.

Jethro hooded his eyes. The smile she was trying out was wobbling round the edges, and anxiety positively shrieked from those wide dark blue eyes. For the first time she looked vulnerable, the calm, cool poise he associated with her wiped away by some trouble or other.

She put a hand up to her mouth, as if to hide the embryo smile that had somehow turned into a shaky grimace, the movement totally at odds with her usual grace, clumsy almost.

He stamped on the urge to fold her in his arms, to tell her to stop worrying about whatever it was that was troubling her because, whatever it was, he'd sort it. She wasn't for him and never could be; she leaned in a different direction entirely.

Because someone, some time, had to say something, he leaned back on his heels and asked flatly, 'Is there something I can do for you?' Then he made a minor production of looking at his watch, as if counting out the seconds he could spare her.

Allie made a huge effort to drag herself together. For heaven's sake, he was only a man, and no man up to now had had the power to intimidate her. This one was no different from the rest. That bleak, tough expression was probably down to nothing more scary than peevishness. He was looking sniffy because she'd consistently turned down his offers of a date.

Well, she could offer him something of far more use to him than a few miserable dates. Money. Lots of it.

She squared her shoulders beneath the cotton shirt she was wearing tucked into baggy green trousers that had been through the wash a couple of dozen times too many—nothing remotely sexy to give him funny ideas—sucked some air into her cramped lungs and managed to say coolly, 'I need a favour, and I'm willing to pay handsomely for it.'

Naming the sum at her disposal, she watched closely for a change in his expression. Nothing, not even the merest flicker of interest. She had been so sure that he would jump at the opportunity of getting his hands on what must seem to him to be a small fortune, and ask questions about the favour he was to do to earn it after, she felt the disappointment hit her like a blow to the pit of her stomach. To be replaced immediately by the sting of irritation.

She was having a hard time getting through to this looming hulk! And for all she knew his dear old granny probably had her ear pinned to the other side of the door. Frustration edged her voice as she enunciated clearly, 'I suggest we go somewhere to talk about it on neutral ground. But before we do, I must tell you that the sum I mentioned can't be increased.' This was in case he was using that poker-player's face in the hope of upping the ante.

The only response to that was the slight, upward drift of one straight sable brow. It incensed her. Why didn't he just say, No thanks, go away, and be done with it?

'If you're not interested, then please say so, and I won't waste any more of your valuable time!'

In a moment she would swing on her heels and storm out in an almighty temper; he knew that. He also knew that he should let her. Seeing her, the only woman he had actively pursued, the one woman who would never give him a second glance, wasn't doing much for his own mood either. The feeling of being an utter jerk was new to him, and he didn't like it.

Just as he'd predicted, she swung round on her heels, angry impatience keeping her shoulders rigid, and he said, 'I'm interested,' then cursed himself for the instinctive words, for not letting her go, getting her out of his sight, out of his head. He qualified his statement when he saw the wash of relief on her face as she turned back to him. 'I'm curious to know what favour you're willing to pay so highly for. Shall we go?'

He left her standing in the hallway for a minute or two, presumably while he went to let his grandmother know he'd be out for a while. Did the old lady demand to be told where he was and what he'd be doing? Was she over-protective because she knew he was feckless, incapable of holding a job down for more than five minutes at a time, was a sandwich short of a picnic?

She couldn't go along with that, not after walking into that room and sensing the aura of power that surrounded him, seeing the cold, clinically distanced look in those golden eyes.

Suddenly she shivered, as if a goose had walked over her grave, and he said from just behind her, 'Ready?'

'If you are,' she replied and fell in step behind him. But she baulked when he opened the passenger door of his dreadful old van. 'I thought we might walk to a park, find a bench to sit on,' she objected. 'There's no need to drive.' The vehicle didn't look as if it would go a hundred yards without braking down, and the thought of being cocooned in it with him made her feel even more nervous. She'd feel easier in the open air, with other things—people and traffic—to provide a distraction.

She planted her feet firmly on the pavement, but he said smoothly, 'And I thought we'd drive out to a pub I know of. It has a garden at the back which overlooks the river. We'll have coffee, and if the conversation proves interesting enough stay on for lunch.' His long mouth curled derisively. 'Or are you afraid that being seen riding in an old banger might spoil your super-model image?'

So he knew! She wasn't going to ask how, but he'd hit a raw nerve. Her mouth tightened. She plucked angrily at her baggy cotton trousers. 'Do you think I'd dress this way if I was afraid of that?' And she inserted herself into the passenger seat, just to show him.

Then she wished she'd stuck to her guns and insisted on walking to a park. Even the rough, grinding sound of the engine did nothing to ease the silence between them. It was all proving to be even more of a strain than she had imagined. Allie really couldn't understand what was happening here. All last week, on the occasions when he'd forced his company on her, he'd been giving off mega-strong signals. He fancied her, wanted to date her, wanted—as they all did—to get her into bed.

And now he was acting as if he thoroughly disliked

her. She'd thought she'd got him taped: feckless, short on cash and prospects, long on male conceit, thinking that he only had to look at a woman in that explicit way he had to have her panting, begging...

He was turning out to be an enigma!

Allie heaved an unconscious sigh and Jethro took his eyes off the road for a moment to glance at her profile. Pure poetry. Smooth, wide forehead, straight, neat nose, the curling upper lip above that invitingly sensual mouth. The fine, delicate skin needed no make-up, and the tender length of her neck, exposed by her scraped back silvery gold hair, made him ache.

He glared back at the road ahead, his jaw tightening. He should have told her he wasn't interested in whatever it was she was prepared to pay him for. Should have let her go. She—although he had to admit she could hardly have meant it, because why should she explain her sexual orientation to someone who was practically a stranger?—had made a fool out of him.

And by being here he was making a fool out of himself.

The knowledge didn't sit easily, and his mouth was grim as he parked the van on the forecourt of the pleasant riverside inn.

Coffee was what they'd come for and coffee was what they'd have. Forget lunch. Why prolong it? He'd find out what was troubling her, give her the best advice he could offer, drive her back and get the hell out. Forget he'd wanted her—still did, dammit!—forget she'd ever existed.

He stalked inside ahead of her, and was digging into his jeans pocket for the money to pay for the coffee he'd ordered when, beside him, she dug into her shoulder bag for her purse and said quietly, 'Let me do this.' She handed a note over the bar counter.

Jethro almost walked out right there and then. He wasn't used to having a woman pay for him, and hated the feeing of being patronised. Before this wretched morning was over he'd tell her who he was, what he was.

A few words from him and she'd realise that the money she'd laid on the table as payment for a favour as yet unspecified might seem like a lot to her but would be considered as nothing more than loose change by him!

Wallowing in the ignoble thought, he gestured to the open French windows which led out to sun-drenched gardens overlooking the Severn and allowed her to precede him. Then he wished the hell he hadn't, because the light shone through the thin fabric of the loose pants she was wearing, clearly delineating every elegant contour of her long and lovely legs.

Battening down an upsurge of lust, he followed her out to the only table with a sun umbrella. It was green, and the shade it cast made her look ethereal. The slender hands that fiddled with stray tendrils of silky hair, tucking them behind her delicate ears, were so fine-boned, almost transparent in their fragility, that they brought a lump to his throat.

It was such a waste!

Firmly, he reminded himself that she could no

more help the way she was than she could help the
shape of her nose, the texture of her skin, the curve
of her mouth.

Such a kissable mouth.

Growling silently at the torture he was inflicting on
himself, he waited until the coffee things had been
brought out to them and then got straight to the point,
because it would be masochistic to spin it out. He
wanted her out of his life—well out of it.

'So, what's the favour you're willing to pay me
for?'

Allie stopped fiddling with her hair and started fiddling with the strap of her bag instead. The moment
had come, and quite frankly she was terrified. This
man would be no push-over, happy to dance to the
tune she arranged for him. This man, with his intim-
idating look of grim-faced power, would do nothing
he didn't want to do—and heaven help anyone who
tried to make him!

But she had already stuck a toe in the metaphorical
water, so she might as well plunge right in.

'I need you to marry me,' she said.

CHAPTER THREE

EVERYTHING inside him lurched. Forty-eight hours ago he'd have jumped at the offer, done practically anything to have her in his life, in his bed. And he knew now, right at this moment, that he would even have been willing to settle for wedding bells and marriage vows for the first time in his life.

Dear Lord, he must have gone and fallen in love! And that was why no other woman had ever given him such intense pleasure to look at, such a charged adrenalin rush, such an aching need—

His hormones really started playing up, mushing up his brain, and he took a long gulp of scalding coffee to quiet them down. All last week she hadn't wanted to know him, had frozen him out with frigid politeness. Now she wanted marriage—and was wiling to *pay* for it!

He looked into her troubled blue eyes, his own skimming down to note the way she was chewing on a corner of her mouth as she waited for him to respond, and said, 'Why? Are you pregnant?'

It was the first explanation that came into his head. Why else would a beautiful woman want a husband, any husband, unless she'd been made pregnant, wanted a father for the coming child because its natural one had run away?

A rosy blush spread from her primly buttoned neckline to the roots of her hair as she repudiated quickly, 'No, of course not!'

Which brought him right back to where he'd started from. Of course not, he thought, deploring his own stupidity. She could hardly get impregnated if her partner wasn't of the opposite gender.

To give himself time to get his head straight he angled away from the table and hooked one arm over the back of the chair, offering her a suave exterior that was completely at odds with the turmoil going on inside him, and prodding, 'Then why don't you tell me why you want to marry? And why pick me?'

Allie was fighting to stay cool, to squash the impulse to get up and run. The laid-back character who had hung around most evenings last week was nothing like the man who was facing her across the table now. This man looked tough, as if he could command huge international armies with the lift of one straight black brow. All sharp edges, and then some.

So how could she tell him that she believed he'd do anything for a hand-out?

Only once this morning had he seemed like the man she had come to know—unwillingly, she reminded herself—and that had been when she'd said she wanted him to marry her. He'd worn the same expression as he had when she'd first thanked him for helping her mother. Shellshocked.

He was waiting, and of course he had a right to hear the reasons for her proposal. To him it must have sounded like the ravings of a lunatic!

His golden eyes were alert, despite his relaxed position. And the way he'd hooked an arm over the back of the chair somehow forced her eyes to where the soft fabric of his T-shirt outlined his overpowering masculinity, those strong wide shoulders, the broad chest that tapered down to a flat, narrow waist.

She bit down on her lip and lowered her eyes. So he was sexy. So what? He was still the same person, struggling to earn a living. So get on with it, woman, spit it out, she exhorted herself, then took a deep breath, laid the palms of her hands flat on the table and told herself she had nothing to lose.

'My uncle, Fabian Brannan, left me a property in Shropshire on condition that I was married at the time of his death or within one month after it. I don't want it, and I certainly don't want to be married.' She raised her eyes to hold his, and there was no disputing the sincerity of that final statement. 'But my mother wants Studley Manor. She spent the happiest years of her life there and she would give anything to be able to go back.'

Her tiny sigh was soft, barely ruffling her breath, but he heard it and, cursing the way she could so easily rouse his protective instincts, intrigue him, he found himself asking softly, 'So why did she leave it?'

'Fabian wanted it back,' she told him, and if she sounded bitter she couldn't help it. 'My grandfather had two sons: Fabian, and Mark, my father. Dad was the youngest by several years, and apparently considered to be a no-account weakling, a hopeless dreamer.

When Grandfather died the family home, Studley Manor, went to Fabian. He had no use for the place, no desire to live in the sticks, and was busy making his fortune in London and living the life of a rake, by all accounts. But he grudgingly agreed to let my parents use it when they knew I was on the way. A five-year lease and a modest rent.

'Dad wrote fiction. Not very successfully, but he earned enough to scrape by. The lack of money didn't matter to them; they were happy—two dreamy romantics living in cloud-cuckoo-land. Crunch time came when I was fifteen. Fabian wanted us out and refused to renew the third lease. Against all our expectations he'd decided to marry, and his future wife had a yen to play Lady of the Manor.'

Her mouth had tightened, he noted. There was a white line around her unpainted lips. 'So you and your parents were out?'

She nodded, picked up the spoon from her saucer and began turning it round and round. Then she dropped it and folded her hands together quickly, as if the nervous gesture had betrayed her. When she spoke again her voice was cool and controlled, and he wondered if she always bottled up her emotions, and what would happen if they were released.

'We left Studley and came to live with my mother's sister. Fran. Her husband had recently walked out on her. We were to stay until Dad could find us a place to rent. I can remember Mother trying to be brave, saying it didn't matter if the place he found was falling down, so long as it was back in the country and had a garden. They were like two bewildered children. Then...' Her voice shook, but she controlled it. 'The publishers Dad had been with for years sold out to one of the big international outfits. They refused to renew his contract. They considered his work to be dated, said it didn't fit the market. Two blows in quick succession. He'd lost our home and he'd lost his only source of income. He wasn't strong enough to take it. He took his own life instead.'

Instinctively Jethro reached over and covered her hands with his own. 'That was tough, Allie.' She made no attempt to draw her hands away and he was glad of that, because all he wanted to give her at this moment was the comfort of caring human contact.

Her fingers unfurled slowly and curled around his, as if she were grateful for the warmth and strength of him. He eased his breath out gently and said, 'Have you considered that although your mother wants to go back, or thinks she does, she might find the memories too painful to bear if it actually happened?'

'Oh, no.' She seemed quite adamant about that; there was even a ghost of a smile playing at the corners of her mouth. 'Two years after Dad died we heard that Studley was empty again. Fabian's wife was suing for divorce, was living in France, and he'd moved back to London. When my mother heard that, it was as if she'd come to life again. She travelled up to see him—she had such plans. I'd left school, and was wondering how to make money fast and legally, and she wanted to go back—believed she and I could start a small nursery in the walled garden, make a go of it. And sure, Fabian told her, we could move back to Studley, do as we pleased with it—provided he got regular ''visiting rights''. He'd always fancied her, thought her too good for his useless wimp of a brother.' Allie shrugged fatalistically. 'So that was that. No dice.'

She looked him full in the face, her deep blue eyes glittering. 'Fulfilling the conditions of his will now would serve two objectives. Giving Laura back her lost happiness, the joy of being where she wants to be, doing what she wants to do. And getting the better of Fabian for once. That,' she told him firmly, 'is why I have to go back to the solicitor within the next three weeks with a husband on my arm.'

'Why me?'

She looked at him blankly, then slowly withdrew her hands from his, as if only now becoming aware of how tightly she'd been holding on to him. 'Because I don't know of any other man who'd consent to the sort of marriage I have in mind,' she told him honestly. His compassion had eased something between them, allowing her to slough off the earlier tension, open up. 'And I figured you might find the money handy.' Dimples appeared at the corners of her mouth. 'You could even buy yourself new transport. Heaven knows, you need it.'

'And what sort of marriage do you have in mind?' He thought he knew, and she confirmed it.

'Nominal. You pick up the money and we put on a united front in public until Studley's legally mine. But behind closed doors it's separate rooms, separate lives. Then, after a decent interval—twelve months, say—you leave me, or I leave you. Irreconcilable differences.'

Twelve months of being bought and paid for, living with her and yet not living with her, knowing there was no way he could make her change her mind about the separate rooms angle because she liked her bread buttered on the other side. It would drive him crazy.

But her desperate need to do what she could to make her mother happy had touched him. She and Laura had had it tough, and he knew exactly what he was going to suggest. Which meant coming clean about who he was.

But first there were a couple of things he had to ask her.

'If you don't marry I take it the property will be sold? If that's the case, why don't you buy it? The money you offered me could go a long way towards a deposit. You could repay the mortgage from your earnings. Top models don't get paid in Monopoly money.'

'True,' she acknowledged tautly. The way he was going round the houses, refusing to give her a definite yes or no, was beginning to wind her up. 'But look at it realistically. At the moment I'm flavour of the month—and it took me years to get there—tomorrow I could be back to catalogue work. I can't risk it. The manor and land could fetch close to a million if it went to auction.'

He dipped his head in silent acknowledgement. In a moment he'd explain what he meant to do: buy this

Studley Manor estate when it came on the open market. After all, property was a no-lose investment. He would install Laura, charge a peanut rent. No strings. No outpourings of gratitude. Nothing. *Finis.*

But first he had to hear confirmation from her own mouth. He had no reason to disbelieve what Laura had said, and one or two remarks Allie had made had reinforced it for him. But he had to hear it from her. Only then could he really get her out of his mind.

'Allie—are you gay?'

Her eyes went wide and dark as she stared at him disbelievingly, then her cheekbones bloomed with colour. 'You conceited bastard! Just because I made it clear I wasn't interested in dating you, and wouldn't have sex with you if we were married, you automatically assume I have to be gay!' She collected her bag, slung the strap over her shoulder and shot to her feet, glaring at him furiously. 'I'm as straight as you are; I just don't happen to fancy you. All I want from you is a piece of paper to prove I'm married.' Her eyes narrowed, her jaw tightened, and she said through her teeth, 'And as you obviously have no intention of obliging me, I'll say goodbye!'

She stalked away, over the lawns, threading her way through the scattered tables, her shoulder bag bumping against her hip.

Jethro watched her, grinning, his white teeth gleaming. Her furious and obviously genuine disclaimer had changed everything. Hadn't it just!

Laura's statement that Allie wasn't interested in men had no roots in her daughter's sexuality. Wary of men, was more like it. Because of something that had happened in her past? He aimed to find out what it was, and change her attitude.

As for her blistering pronouncement that she didn't fancy him and would insist on separate rooms should they marry—well, that was something else he intended to change!

Slowly he got to his feet, turned his grin on the openly curious middle-aged couple at the nearest table, dug into his pocket for a handsome tip, dropped it on the tray and casually followed in Allie's turbulent wake.

He had every intention of obliging the lady!

And no intention whatsoever of expecting anything other than an ecstatically happy outcome!

CHAPTER FOUR

ALLIE stood on the forecourt of the fashionable riverside inn and the sun beat down on her head. The
entire morning had been an unmitigated disaster. Not
only had Jethro Conceited Cole made it pretty damn
clear that he wasn't interested in her offer, but she
had put paid to any hope of being able to persuade
him to change his mind because she had done the
unprecedented and lost her temper, practically snap-
ping his head off his shoulders! She didn't know how
or why it had happened. Her colleagues didn't call
her Ms Cucumber for nothing!

Any chance she now had of inheriting Studley had
gone right down the drain.

She really didn't know how she was going to face
her mother and tell her that there was now no chance
of getting Studley back. She shouldn't have allowed
the poor dear to hope. And she shouldn't have lied to
that solicitor in the first place.

Her spine wilting, her spirits as flat as yesterday's
champagne, she dismissed the idea of walking back
to town along five or so miles of hot dusty road,
turned to go back into the inn to phone for a taxi, and
walked straight into the solid wall of Jethro's broad
chest.

Every last gasp of air left her body as she felt his

steadying arms go round her, felt the warmth of his body burn through to her skin, making her tremble, every nerve-end suddenly alight with something that felt suspiciously like the tension of high excitement. She put a hand up to push him away, felt the beat of his heart beneath her palm, felt the heat of him, and weakly left her hand precisely where it was, because she'd somehow lost the strength to move it.

'Ready to go?'

The husky, honeyed softness of his voice, the feather-light caress of his breath against her over-heated temple, finally got through to her. Heaven only knew how long they'd been standing like this, like lovers who couldn't bear to break bodily contact!

As his hands slid down, down to her waist, and showed every indication of going lower, his touch growing ever more intimate, she sprang away and felt her pulse begin a hectic beat at the base of her throat.

'I'm going—' Horrified, she realised she sounded like a strangled hen and, worse, he was grinning at her, a particularly piratical kind of grin. She swallowed convulsively as she scrambled for her famous dignity and managed more or less calmly to finish what she'd started to say, 'I'm going to phone for a taxi. There's no need for you to waste any more of your time.'

'My time's my own,' he told her lightly, his golden eyes dancing beneath the thick black frame of his lashes, 'and I'll use it any way I please.' He used one hand to push a soft dark lick of hair out of his eyes, the other to cup her elbow. Tightly. 'My future wife doesn't ride in taxis while I'm around to drive her.'

Allie felt her feet grow roots through the gravel, felt her breath grow tight and heavy in her lungs. If she'd heard him correctly, and she knew she had, then she should be dragging him back inside, treating him to the best champagne the inn could offer, celebrating having beaten Fabian at his own game.

So why wasn't she? Why this feeling of deep, paralysing apprehension, as if her future was no longer hers to order and arrange? As if everything that made her life pleasant and predictable had changed, and nothing would ever be the same again.

Just shock, she told herself staunchly. She hadn't been expecting this, had already resigned herself to failure. So his compliance had stunned her. Nothing odd about that. She'd be fine in a minute.

'Shall we go?' He removed his hand from her elbow, reaching into the pocket of his jeans for the ignition keys, and Allie ran the tip of her tongue over parched lips. She felt the warmth of that small physical contact recede, leaving her skin suddenly icy cold.

She shivered convulsively as he led the way to his van, which looked even more decrepit parked amongst the shiny family saloons, one or two nippy-looking drop-head coupés. And she knew she had to find the voice that seemed to have gone missing and say something to show him she was grateful. Surely she should at least be feeling gratitude, instead of this strange sensation of standing on shifting sands?

But he saved her the effort of trying to find something sensible to say because as soon as the engine
was running, after a few tired-sounding coughs, he
told her, 'I'll take you home. I expect you'll want to
break the news to Laura and Fran when they get back
from work. You'll think of something to tell them to
explain the suddenness? And I'll get the ceremony
sorted—I take it you won't want a flashy wedding?
There wouldn't be time to arrange one even if you
did,' he said matter-of-factly. 'A civil ceremony, I
would imagine. As our marriage is to be short-lived—
twelve months, I think you decided?—it would be
hypocritical to make vows we have no intention of
keeping in church. Agreed?'

'Yes, of course.' His sensitivity took her by surprise and she wondered why it should, because she
knew nothing about his character except that he'd
been kind to her mother when she'd needed help. So
that made two pluses in his favour. She steeled herself
to ask the question that could bring it up to three.

Fixing her eyes on the curling road ahead of them,
she got the words out. 'And you do accept that our
marriage will be in name only?'

Jethro gave her a sideways glance. She looked nervous, her profile taut, her fingers twisted round her
seatbelt as if she were trying for dear life to hold onto
something solid. He said easily, 'Of course. I got that
message loud and clear.' And he added silently, In
name only, sweetheart, until you change your mind!
And believe me, you will. I'll make damn sure of that
if it's the last thing I do!

His eyes back on the road ahead, he could sense her begin to relax. But there was a long way to go. This was only the beginning and, fingers crossed, she was taking the first step towards trusting him. Then, trusting him, she would grow to like him, and a whole new ball game could come from that.

'Thank you,' she said simply, her fingers loosening their clutch on her seatbelt, and was silent for the remainder of the journey. But Jethro knew her mind was buzzing. Elation at having bested her uncle, having found a way round the condition he'd put on her inheritance, plans for the immediate future, what she'd say to her mother and aunt to explain her headlong rush into matrimony.

He knew what was going on in her mind without her having to say a word. He had never been so tuned in to another human being in his life.

Alissa Brannan was his woman, his other half. Subconsciously he must have known that since the first time he'd seen her. His heart squeezed tight. Hell, it was going to be difficult keeping his hands off her when he only had to look at her and his body went into full mating mode, his heart urging him with every beat to tell her how much he loved her.

Fortunately his mind was still functioning well enough to issue instructions to his body about biding his time. He knew they were a perfect match but she didn't. Not yet. But she would. And he could wait, because he always got what he wanted in the end.

As the van juddered to a stop outside Fran's house Allie tried to switch off the thoughts that were flittering around inside her head. She realised ashamedly that she hadn't said a word to him since he'd put her mind at rest and agreed that their marriage wouldn't be consummated. He'd sold her a year of his life, and all she had done for the past twenty minutes was ignore him.

'Come in. I'll fix us some lunch.' The strength of her sudden impulse to make amends took her by surprise. She shouldn't have a guilty conscience, though. Why should she, when she was paying him handsomely for his part in this—this business? And that was what it was. A business arrangement.

Besides, there was so much they had to discuss. 'We have plans to make—the others won't be back until around five-thirty, so we'll have plenty of time. And I can give you that cheque.'

She already had the door of the van open, one foot on the pavement, her stomach fluttering with nervous excitement, with the enormity of what was actually happening. She was going to get Studley back for her mother! And Jethro Cole was willing to help her. She owed him a lunch, the best she could contrive—

'Sorry, but I'll have to pass on that.' His drawled refusal to go along with her suggestion had her plopping back in the seat, her head tipped slightly to one side as she looked at him with huge bewildered eyes. The man who had hung around her most evenings last week would have jumped at the invitation, and besides, if he was as strapped for cash as he appeared to be, she would have thought he'd be more than eager to get his hands on the pay-off. The money, after all, was the only reason he'd agreed to help her.

He angled himself in his seat and stamped on the urge to raise his hand and smooth away the slight frown from between those beautiful deep blue eyes with the tips of his fingers. 'I nccd to find the registrar's office,' he told her evenly, 'and arrange a date and time for the ceremony. I don't know how these places work, but we don't want to run the risk of finding they're fully booked for the time-span we're interested in. And I would imagine we'll need our birth certificates, wouldn't you? Is yours here, or back in London?'

For a moment she looked as if she didn't know what he was talking about, as if events were going far too quickly for her to grasp, and then she nodded. 'It's here. My mother keeps all the official family stuff in a box in her bedroom.'

He smothered a sigh of relief. Getting his hands on his own would present no problem. He'd contact his senior PA. James Abbott had duplicate keys to his Mayfair home and to the safe where his personal documents were kept. He could hop on an Inter-City and be here in next to no time—quicker than if he came up by road. Had hers been kept back in her London apartment it might have meant a delay to the start of what he fully intended to be their future life together.

'Then I suggest you fetch it for me. If I've got it handy, it could save a lot of to-ing and fro-ing.'

Allie reluctantly did as she was told. She supposed it made sense, but she wasn't comfortable with it.

This was *her* grand plan, *her* parade, yet he was the one dishing out the orders.

She ran lightly back down the stairs, clutching the document. This was her wedding, too; she should have a part in fixing the date of the ceremony. She would go with him. Simple. Who had ever heard of the bride not being consulted over a decision like that?

She skidded to a halt in the tiny hallway, her face going pink. She wasn't going to be a bride, not a proper one, and why was she so suddenly wondering what it would be like to be a real one, with a groom as out-and-out sexy as Jethro Cole?

Unsuccessfully willing her overheated skin to cool down, the butterflies to stop attacking her stomach, she went out to where he was waiting in his van. Jerking open the passenger door, she told him, 'I'm coming with you. We should be together when we fix the date.'

There was a stubborn set to her chin, belied, though, by the look of slightly anxious bemusement deep in her eyes, by the pinkness of her skin that was steadily turning to scarlet. The cool, classy, keep-your-distance woman of a week ago had thawed into someone with feelings, real emotions.

A sting of elation flared inside him, but he reminded himself it was early days. She had shown him a tiny crack in her coolly controlled façade, and it was up to him to widen it until there was no going back. But gently.

Her decision to accompany him was entirely natural, and for a moment he was tempted. But only for a moment. The need to have her with him, never let her out of his sight, was hot, visceral, a fist around his heart, but he told her, 'It's best you stay here and work out what you're going to say to Laura. I can't think she'd be happy to know the truth—that you're handing over what probably amounts to your entire savings, tying yourself up with a virtual stranger, just to get her what she thinks she wants.'

He leaned over and plucked the document from her fingers, turned the key in the ignition. 'So think about it. I'll drop by this evening, around seven, and we can discuss the fine print. And another thing—never offer payment in advance. You never know, you could be taken for a ride. I'll take your money, but only after we've both signed on the dotted line.'

He drove away, leaving her standing on the pavement, and he hated having to do it. Making arbitrary decisions for other people was part of his successful boardroom technique—second nature. But using it with her left a sour taste in his mouth.

But he had no option in this instance. He had to contact James Abbott, and then tell Nanny Briggs and Harry they were welcome to dance at his wedding provided they kept quiet about his identity and showed no surprise whatsoever if Allie referred to them as Granny and Gramps!

And he had to persuade Harry to let him borrow this wreck of a van for the duration, arrange for the safe-keeping of his Jag for an indefinite period, contact the gardener and housekeeper at his country home and tell them to make themselves scarce for the next couple of weeks. He could do none of this if Allie was with him.

The fiction of the down-at-heel, feckless character with a losing streak had to be maintained. If she knew who he really was, that the sum she'd offered for his part in the deception had hardly more relevance to him than the loose change in his pocket, she would know he had an ulterior motive in agreeing to be her husband, bought and paid for.

And she would call the whole thing off, Studley or no Studley.

That, he told himself firmly, was not going to happen.

CHAPTER FIVE

LAURA arrived home much earlier than Allie had expected. She had watched Jethro drive away with a totally unwarranted feeling of abandonment, and spent the intervening half an hour trying to talk herself out of that ridiculous state of mind, foolishly letting her thoughts dwell exclusively on him instead of deciding how to break the news of her imminent marriage to a hunky but apparently feckless window-cleaner.

And now her mother was here, and Allie didn't have a clue about how she was going to dress the news up to make it sound believable.

'I cancelled this afternoon's stint with Mrs Thompson,' Laura explained, perching on a stool at the breakfast bar and pushing a limp strand of hair away from her forehead. 'She wasn't too pleased, but that can't be helped. I suddenly realised it's not fair on you, leaving you kicking your heels here while I'm working all hours—especially when you've put your career on hold to spend some time with me. I thought we might do something together this afternoon—look round the shops, if you like, maybe take in a film, if there's anything on you fancy seeing. But first I could murder a cup of tea.'

Grasping the momentary reprieve, Allie turned to

fill the kettle at the sink, reach the teapot and a couple of mugs from the wall cupboard. Her mother looked as downtrodden as a pair of old socks. She wasn't frail, and at forty-one she certainly wasn't old. It was spiritual weariness that was oppressing her, the drudgery of the work she had to do to scrape a living, the feeling she must have that there was no light at the end of the tunnel.

Well, that was going to change. Allie poured boiling water onto the leaves in the pot, her chest filling with the need to tell her everything was going to be fine. But she knew she had to hold back and make the acquisition of Studley sound like a very secondary consideration.

Allie had never lied to her mother, but she was going to have to now. Jethro had been perfectly right when he'd said Laura would be unhappy with the truth. Her mother had always been a hopeless romantic—from an early age Allie had recognised that both her parents had lived with their heads in the clouds—and she would view marrying for the sole purpose of material gain, even if that gain was Studley, as being totally distasteful.

She would never be completely content back at her beloved Studley if she knew the price her daughter had paid to get it for her.

The tea poured, chocolate digestives laid out on a plate, there was no longer an excuse for delay. Allie cleared her throat nervously, avoided her mother's eyes, and stated, 'I've got something to tell you.'

'Something nice?' Laura was nibbling a biscuit,

spooning sugar into her tea at the same time. She had the type of metabolism that allowed her to pack in the calories and not gain an ounce, and Allie had inherited that enviable trait. But right now she didn't think she'd ever want to eat again.

'I think so!' Allie tried to sound the way she imagined an excitedly fluttery bride-to-be would sound. She knew she'd failed miserably when Laura responded, 'From where I'm sitting, it doesn't look like it. You look as if you're about to confess to breaking every last piece of Fran's best china!'

There was no easy way to lead up to this, so Allie stretched her mouth into a smile and stated, 'I'm going to be married.'

'Married?' Laura repeated, and dropped the second biscuit she was about to take back onto the plate. 'You? You always insisted that getting married and settling down was the last thing you were interested in.' The slight shoulders went rigid beneath the plain grey cotton blouse she was wearing. 'Has it anything to do with that stupid condition of your uncle's?' she questioned grimly. 'When you told me you thought you knew of a way to get our old home back I imagined you'd consult with your own solicitor, see if you could overturn his will because that condition was ridiculous.'

Laura slid down from the stool and carried her mug over to the sink. 'So if you're thinking of overturning your convictions and getting married to see me back at Studley, then forget it. Because I promise you I'll never set foot in the place if you do!'

She held the mug under the fierce gush of the hot water tap and scrubbed at it as if she aimed to wash the pattern clean off the surface, and Allie knew she had to act her socks off. Her mother hadn't even asked whom she was marrying—that was how little she believed in her daughter's sudden desire to rush to the altar!

Willing herself to get it right, she went and hugged the older woman, made herself giggle. 'Are you nuts? I know how much you long for the old place, but there are limits to what I'd do to help you get back there, and prostituting myself is one of them!'

She hated lying to her mother. Hated it! But what else could she do when the poor dear's future contentment was at stake? And at least she wasn't lying about the prostitution part, because Jethro wouldn't lay a finger on her. It was part of the agreement.

Laura would never find out that the marriage had been a means to an end, a business contract, and for her own part, being legally tied to Jethro for a year would be nothing more than a vague nuisance. A small price to pay.

She knew her words had penetrated her mother's suspicions when she shrugged the hugging arms away and turned to fix Allie with a very determined eye.

'If you tell me the ceremony's due to take place within the next three weeks then I'll know I'm right. So look me in the eye and tell me it isn't!'

'Of course it is.' Allie injected a note of exasperation. 'It's called killing two birds with one stone!' Then she added, more gently, 'We would have waited a little longer, given ourselves time to have a wedding with all the trimmings. But not much longer, because we would have married before my next shoot in any case. So we thought about it and decided to set a date some time within the next three weeks. So we get each other and you get Studley and everyone's happy—except possibly, Fabian, who will be looking down on us and gnashing his teeth!'

'So who's the lucky man? Do I know him?'

Laura still looked far from convinced, and no doubt would look totally sceptical when she learned who her future son-in-law would be. Allie bit the bullet. 'Of course you do. It's Jethro Cole.' And, to her amazement, she watched a lot of the suspicious tightness leach out of her mother's face.

'The window-cleaner?' she queried, as if to make sure there weren't two Jethro Coles she ought to know about.

'That's the one,' Allie responded. 'Don't tell me you think a mere window cleaner is beneath me!'

A sudden mental image of Jethro's hard, very male naked body beneath her own equally naked, much softer one sent a violent rush of blood to her face, staining her ivory cheeks a vivid scarlet. But at least she now had her mother on the defensive instead of the attack, because no one could accuse Laura Brannan of snobbishness and hope to get away with it.

'Of course not! I never despise an honest day's work, whatever it is—I would have thought you knew me better than that! And you can tell just by looking at him that he's more determined than most. He'll probably end up with his own window-cleaning empire.'

'And he's very sexy with it!' Allie put in, and wondered where those words had come from. And why. But her subconscious mind must have told her they were necessary, because for the first time since she'd dropped her bombshell Laura's eyes were twinking.

'So you noticed?' she commented drily. 'The way you always looked through him, I assumed you hadn't. I knew he was smitten, the way he called round on any pretext—or no pretext at all—the way he couldn't take his eyes off you. But you always froze him off. The last time I saw him I took pity on him and told him he was wasting his time because you weren't interested in men.'

So that was why he'd wondered if she was gay! Not, as she'd thought, because of his monumental male conceit. A lilt of pleasure she didn't bother to question stole into her heart, and she let it stay there because it made her feel good. He hadn't been speaking out of the kind of crass male vanity that made a man call a woman gay just because she didn't want to go to bed with him. She had maligned his character when she'd thought it.

'So?' Laura prodded. 'What made you change your mind so suddenly?'

'I thawed! We met up this morning and we went for coffee, and—' Oh, Lordy, Laura was never going to buy it. Falling in love, supposedly, and deciding to marry after knowing the man for only a week and giving him the cold shoulder for all of that time. Then, on a sudden burst of inspiration, she continued, 'I don't know if you're going to believe this, but it was like a bolt of lightning. I just knew he was the only man in the world who could matter to me.'

It wasn't an out-and-out falsehood, not really. He had become the man most important to her by virtue of her not knowing another who would be willing to let her buy a year of his life! But she seemed, as she had hoped, to have punched the right button. Her mother, the perennial romantic, hugged her, all smiles now.

'Why wouldn't I believe you? It happened just like that for your father and me!'

'Did you find the glasses?' Allie asked her mother several hours later. 'Jethro should be here any time now.'

'They're in the kitchen and the champagne's in the fridge. Should I pop out to the corner shop and get some nuts for nibbles?'

Excitement made Laura look like a young girl again. Her daughter had fallen head over heels in love at last and was marrying a man she herself thoroughly liked. And as a bonus she would be able to live at Studley, again, put all those dreams of a nursery garden into practice.

'No,' Allie said firmly. 'No nibbles. Just a glass of champagne, then Jethro and I will be off—we do need to spend the evening on our own.' She pressed her fingertips to her aching forehead as Fran, sitting on the chair near the window and apparently absorbed in the evening newspaper, snorted derisively.

She had to get Jethro out of here and become herself again. Cool, in control, distant. She didn't need to play-act for him, thank heaven.

She was pleased, of course she was, with the way she'd handled this very tricky situation. Laura now believed that she and Jethro, whom she had liked on sight, ever since he'd picked her up off the pavement, were besottedly in love, and was happy. And this afternoon they'd gone to the shops, because that was what Allie had believed was expected of her, and chosen something to wear for the ceremony, because Allie had said she had nothing suitable with her and Laura had commented that she had nothing suitable full stop.

Watching her mother come really alive as they had tried on hats, Allie had known that she'd got everything right. It had been hard to pretend an interest, discuss the comparative merits of a classic little suit in deep blue silk and a simple shift dress in bronze-coloured linen topped by matching straight-line jacket when she'd known all the time that the blue silk would do, that anything, provided it wasn't a pair of jeans and a T-shirt, would do.

But the hardest part was still to come: acting the part of a woman who was besottedly in love in front of the scornful Fran and the doting Laura. Already the palms of her hands felt damp with perspiration and her heart was racing.

Fran put her newspaper aside and made a big production of looking at her watch.

'He's late.'

'Only by ten minutes,' Laura responded tartly. She still hadn't forgiven her sister for her reaction to the news.

'God save us, Allie,' she had snorted. 'Have you gone mad? You hardly know the man. He's probably heard of your earning power. He'll stick around for a couple of years, grab all the goodies he can, and then dump you. He's got a fantastic body, I'll give you that, and if you want to go to bed with him, go ahead. You don't have to marry him, for pity's sake!'

Ten more minutes ticked by with excruciating slowness, and Allie knew that if Fran didn't stop looking at her watch every few seconds, if her mother plumped the cushions or tweaked the curtains one more time, she would scream!

Suddenly her mood changed from taut annoyance to dragging, draining defeat. He wasn't going to come. He'd chickened out. All her plans were going pear-shaped.

So when he did walk in off the street, looking too handsome for his own good, her relief was so great she didn't have to tell herself to give him a smile of welcome, it just came.

He looked so good. The fresh white T-shirt he was wearing emphasised the taut lines of his upper body and deepened the tanned, olive tones of his skin, and his legs looked even longer and leaner in semi-respectable black denim jeans that fitted his narrow hips and excessively masculine backside like a second skin.

If he was aware of Fran's frosty expression he didn't show it. He accepted Laura's hug and bubbly congratulations with the laid-back grace and charm he seemed able to produce at will, and then advanced on Allie, whose heart was beating so fiercely she was sure everyone in the room would be able to hear it.

'Miss me, sweetheart?' The smooth, dark-honey tones oozed confidence, a supreme self-assuredness that made an apology for his lateness unthinkable. A lean, long-fingered hand was clamped against her narrow waist as he tugged her into the heat of his body and her heart began a fluttery dance of panic.

There was no escaping the intimacy he was forcing on her. Not while they were in the same room as her mother and her aunt. She would just have to grin and bear it and remind herself that he, too, was acting a part, that the wicked gleam in his eyes was nothing to do with the way their bodies were glued together and everything to do with the fat cheque he was well on his way to earning.

After they'd taken a sip of the champagne Laura had decided was obligatory they'd be out of here at the speed of light—she'd make sure of that—and in the meantime she'd simply imagine she was being hugged by the big brother she'd never had.

But that was before he kissed her.

Firm fingers curled around her chin, lifting her face, and before she knew what was happening he bent his dark head and feathered his lips over her mouth, his tongue tasting and moulding the lush contours.

Allie gasped as raw sensation exploded inside her and spread like quickfire into every inch of her body. And when he took advantage of her helplessly parted lips and sought a much deeper intimacy her head felt as if it were about to spin off her shoulders. The bones in her legs gave way, so she had no choice but to cling onto him, wrapping her arms around his neck...

'Champagne, my darlings—or are you already floating six feet above the ground?'

Saved by Laura, her bottle and her glasses, Allie thought muzzily, resisting the impulse to scrub the back of her hand over the mouth that had recently been so very thoroughly plundered. She didn't know what had come over her. Normally she would never dream of letting a man near her that way. It could only lead further and further into a sexual trap, and Allie Brannan would never knowingly put herself in that kind of danger.

But now wasn't normal; it was fantasy, a charade—and *necessary*, she reminded herself. Totally necessary if her mother were to believe the web of lies she'd spun. And the way his kiss had made her feel—out of it and wanting it never to stop, wanting more, so much more—had to be nothing but reaction to the tension of the endless day, to the belief, towards the end, that he'd reneged on their bargain.

'Would you do the honours, Jethro?' Laura held out the unwieldy bottle. 'I'm not very good at it.'

Fran got out of her chair. 'Here, let me. He's already got his hands full,' she said drily. 'A pity to spoil love's young dream when it normally doesn't outlast the honeymoon.'

Ignoring her aunt's acid comments was far easier than ignoring the way Jethro's hands were pressed into the small of her back, moulding her closer into his body. She gave him a surreptitious shove, shakily reached for a glass, and croaked, 'Only a taste for me, Fran.'

She had to get them out of here, and fast. Then he could stop playing to the gallery. At once. No more touching, no more kissing. Then she would be back on firm ground and the annoying haze would clear from her eyes. At the moment it was like looking at everything through a gently swaying gauze curtain.

'Only a drop for me, too,' Jethro said regretfully, and Allie heaved a silent sigh of relief because he, too, wanted out of this necessary charade. 'I haven't eaten since breakfast.'

'Oh, Allie! How could you? You expressly told me not to keep supper back, that Jethro would have already eaten.' Laura stopped scolding her daughter and turned a motherly smile on her future son-in-law. 'It will take me five minutes to make an omelette— which would you prefer, mushroom or cheese?'

He felt the soft, melting curves of Allie's body go rigid against his, heard the soft hiss of her quickly indrawn breath, felt her hold it. It was tempting—so tempting—to accept the offer, to spin out his visit because his prickly Allie had no option but to play the part of his besotted future wife in front of her family.

And touching her like this, holding her fantastic body against his, feeling the sweet, feminine softness of her, tasting her lips, was a need that had been driving him wild since he'd met up with her again. The beauty of it had been her unwitting response to him, the yielding softness of her parted lips, the sudden stab of sexual awareness he had felt through the barrier of clothing that had separated their heated bodies.

But that response was enough for now. More than enough. Prolonging this enforced intimacy would only make her resent him, and he never, ever took a backward step.

He reached for her hands, took them in his, gave her a soft, conspiratorial smile. 'Thanks, Laura. But Allie and I will pick up a snack in town.' He watched the tension drain from her lovely face, saw her kissable lips relax into a tiny smile, and that was adequate compensation—for the moment, anyway—for denying himself the physical closeness the situation here demanded she accept.

Then he drawled, in his own private, wicked retaliation, 'We've got a helluva lot to thrash out. I got a special licence and the wedding's fixed for three o'clock tomorrow afternoon.'

Fully aware of the stunned silence, he swept her mother and her aunt with laughing golden eyes. 'I hope you two ladies will be able to make it, give us your blessings when we tie the knot!'

CHAPTER SIX

'ARE you sure this thing's capable of getting us there?' Allie questioned suspiciously as she hiked the short, tight skirt of the blue silk suit she'd been married in up to her thighs, to allow her to slide reluctantly into the passenger seat of his deplorable old van. She had very little inclination to embark on a pretend honeymoon, and even less to spend the first part of it in a broken-down vehicle in the back of beyond.

Jethro tore his eyes away from the elegant, silk-clothed length of her legs and smothered a groan. This was his wedding day, and this gorgeous, shatteringly sexy lady was his bride. Not that she looked at it in quite that way, of course. But she would, he vowed—he'd make damn sure of that!

'It goes,' he said, the dry, almost strangulated tone of his voice the result of his ferocious internal battle with his far too lively hormones. 'Not quickly, and certainly not elegantly. But it goes.'

Harry had been—in his own words—'totally gobs-macked' when he'd been asked for the loan of the van. Why drive the poor girl on her honeymoon in that clapped-out old thing when he had a brand-new Jaguar gathering dust? had been the gist of his stupefaction.

Nanny Briggs, too, had had a whole welter of objections: 'Why the unseemly haste to the altar? Why pretend you're not who you are? And why am I supposed to be your grandmother? I don't like it, Master Jethro. It all sounds very underhand to me, and to my certain knowledge you were never that.'

Thankfully, though, they'd behaved themselves at the short civil ceremony—if looking bewildered constituted good behaviour. Laura, bless her, had been openly ecstatic, wiping motherly tears of joy from her eyes with the corner of a handkerchief. The only sour note had been played by that Fran woman. He didn't know why she'd taken time off from work to attend the ceremony if all she'd been able to do was scowl.

And now the wedding party, such as it was, had dispersed, the suitcases were in the back of the van and they were heading for what was probably one of the strangest honeymoons in history.

He put the van in motion and heard Allie heave a sigh. His heart clenched. He would have much preferred an enormous splash of a wedding and the opportunity to proudly show his beautiful bride to the whole world, instead of a hole-and-corner civil affair that had been over in what had seemed like seconds.

He wanted to whisk her away to some secluded exotic island, shower her with gifts, make love to her until neither of them knew where they were at. He wanted to hang diamonds around her graceful neck and clothe her slender fingers with precious stones and gleaming gold. That thin band of brass—the cheapest he'd been able to find—was a paltry thing, an insult to her heart-wrenching beauty, a miserable denial of what she meant to him.

But if his plan to make her fall in love with the man he was, rather than with his millions, was to have any hope of working, then, as Nanny Briggs would have said, he'd have to let want be his master.

'We don't have to do this,' she said in the cool tones that told him that the fluster brought on by the kissing, stroking and holding of last evening was buried well in the past as far as she was concerned. 'It was good of your friend to say you could borrow his holiday cottage, but as it won't be a real honeymoon I don't see the point. So why don't we head back to London instead? We did agree we'd share my flat for the duration of the marriage. In any case, we have to present ourselves, and the marriage certificate, at Fabian's solicitors.'

'Plenty of time for that,' he stated unequivocally. 'You can phone for an appointment from the cottage; you've got all of three weeks to wave the thing under his nose and claim your inheritance.' The engine rattled and coughed as he negotiated the huge traffic island on the by-pass and pointed the battle-scarred bonnet west.

No way were they heading back to her place.

Last night, after they'd escaped from her family, she'd described her flat as 'tiny'. One small bedroom, more like a cupboard, really, but there was a sofa-bed arrangement in the living room and he could sleep on that. She used it herself on the rare occasions when

Laura came to visit, and it wasn't really that uncomfortable.

He could live with a flat of shoe-box proportions, sleep on a lumpy sofa contraption—no problem. If he had to take up residence in a dustbin to be with her, he'd do so gladly. But once back in London, on her home territory, she'd take herself off, make herself scarce; he knew she would. Once the business with the solicitor was over she'd be lunching with her agent, getting back into the swing of things, and before he knew it she'd be off on a shoot on the other side of the world, putting as much distance as she could between herself and her unwanted but unfortunately necessary husband.

He needed a couple of weeks, just the two of them alone together, to get her to change her mind about his role in her life—and when he'd accomplished that, sofa-beds and separate lives would be the last thing she'd want.

'Think about it,' he said smoothly. 'I already told Laura that my old school-mate offered us the use of his country hideaway. I said we'd be there for a couple of weeks and she has the phone number, remember. She'll start to get suspicious if she tries to contact us and can't, and then discovers we passed up the opportunity of a free honeymoon in rural isolation.'

He had a point, Allie conceded sinkingly. They must do nothing to make her mother suspect that this marriage was anything other than a true love-match. They couldn't do a single thing to rock the boat until the fat lady sang. And that wouldn't happen until

Laura was safely back at Studley and ready to believe, twelve months down the road, that the marriage simply hadn't worked out.

It was the 'rural isolation' bit that made her toes curl. Back in London she could stay out of his way for most of the time, start her career moving again, get involved in her work, take charge of herself for a change. Ever since he'd agreed to marry her he'd been the one taking control—fixing the wedding up so quickly, telling Laura that there was no point in hanging round since they knew they were going to spend the rest of their lives together, apparently contacting an old schoolfriend to ask for the use of his cottage because, as he'd said, he couldn't afford the South of France or a Caribbean island, not on what he earned as a fledgling window-cleaner.

'How isolated?' she asked, hating the note of apprehension in her voice, trying to assure herself that there was nothing to get paranoid about because they had a non-consummation pact, didn't they? He wouldn't try anything on, would he? And the way she'd turned to a jelly when he'd kissed her and held her had been down to nervous tension.

Hadn't it?

'Not a neighbour in sight,' he answered blithely. 'Just the birds and the bees and the butterflies.'

Wrong—all the butterflies in creation had taken residence in her tummy. 'Won't you get terribly bored?' she suggested, out of sheer desperation. 'With nothing to do?'

And she shuddered when a million electric sparks

bombarded her spine as he turned briefly to her, his mouth a sensual curve, his golden eyes heart-crashingly wicked as he murmured softly, 'I'll find something. You can bet a year's earnings on that.'

Wisely, Allie shut her mouth, and kept it shut for the next twenty-odd miles. He hadn't actually meant anything, even though his eyes had been definitely carrying a come-to-bed message. He was just teasing, winding her up, having fun at her expense.

She hoped he wouldn't keep it up during the coming two weeks. It would drive her crazy if he did! And she was not going to ask herself why that should be.

He broke the lengthy silence. 'Almost there.' They were inching down a steep gradient now, down an unmade track with grass growing along the centre and high leafy hedgerows almost meeting overhead, cutting out the sunlight. Welsh border country, and, as the crow flew, not too far from Studley. Romantic country.

She didn't want to think of romantic, but couldn't help it when the final bend brought them to a high garden wall with an arched opening that gave them a glimpse of a stone-built cottage, very much larger than she'd expected, with roses sprawling round the wide oak door and dozens of tiny-paned mullioned windows that twinkled in the late afternoon light.

'It's beautiful!' Despite being dead set against coming here at all, Allie couldn't quash the exclamation of delight. From what she could see of the obviously extensive gardens Jethro's friend favoured the rampageous cottage style, and if she craned her neck she got a glimpse of an archway in the high stone boundary wall which framed a tantalising vista of meadows, trees and distant rolling hills.

A perfect place to spend a week or two soaking up the peace, wallowing in the serenity of the Garden of Eden before the Fall—but there wasn't going to be a fall, she reminded herself when her body went into high-tension mode as Jethro strolled round from the rear of the van to open the passenger door at her side.

If he touched her he would spoil it all, shatter the trance-like peace of this magical place. She held her breath and her skin prickled with the tightness of expectancy and apprehension, because after that charade last evening in front of Laura and Fran she knew that his slightest touch was capable of starting a major riot inside her.

But he made no move to help her out, simply held the door open, reaching for the two suitcases he'd fetched from the rear while she'd been lost in admiration of the property, and left her to it.

Left her to unwillingly admire his back view as he carried the cases towards the cottage door. Somehow he'd managed to find time to buy a suit in honour of the occasion. It certainly looked brand-new, and very definitely off-the-peg. But the poor cut and inexpensive fabric did nothing to detract from the superb body beneath, or the fluid, macho grace of the way that body moved.

Allie gulped around the rock that had suddenly

taken up residence in her throat and reluctantly followed.

Jethro unlocked the heavy oak door, reclaimed the suitcases and pushed his way in, and hoped to heaven his staff had absorbed his telephoned orders and would follow them to the letter. Any slip-up could ruin his long-term plans.

He had no worries as far as Jim, his gardener, was concerned. Practical, reliable, unquestioning, *male*, old Jim wouldn't come near the property for the next two weeks because his boss had told him not to. But Ethel, his housekeeper, who kept the cottage spick and span during his lengthy absences, would be itching to know why she'd been instructed to fully stock the deep-freeze, fridge, larder and wine racks and then make herself scarce for a couple of weeks.

He wouldn't put it past her to be hovering around, ostensibly just on her way out after carrying out his orders and stocking up on food and wine, her black eyes sparking with feminine curiosity as she waited to see just why he wanted this place entirely to himself, and who, if anyone, he was bringing with him.

Unapologetic for the sexism of his thoughts, he strode through to the kitchen, relieved to find it innocent of any avidly curious female presence, and then went back to collect Allie, who was still hovering in the hall, twisting the tawdry wedding band round and round on her slender finger.

His heart twisted with compassion. The poor darling was wired up with nerves, had lost that fabled cool, touch-me-not persona that had been—as he'd discovered to his cost—bone-deep, not merely a trademark.

She glanced up, saw him, and tried to smile. It wobbled alarmingly, and she settled for chewing on her lush lower lip. And he asked himself why? Why so apprehensive? She'd successfully frozen off all his early attempts to date her, get to know her, and, apart from a couple of understandable glitches, which could be put down to a natural distaste for having to ask him to go through a form of marriage for mutual financial gain, she had been calm and collected right up until he'd touched her, kissed her.

So maybe he'd stripped away one of the layers from around her heavily protected heart. Maybe his own yearning need for her had been transmitted through the heated touch of their lips. And maybe she had felt herself respond to it and was terrified, because she could feel her steely lack of interest in matters sexual slipping away.

Sounded logical to him. Elation punched through his gut, clear through to his backbone, and brought an idiotic grin to his face which he quickly subdued. Down boy, he told himself sternly. Take it easy, nice and easy...

The thought of making love to her in precisely that way—easy, nice and easy—not rushing her, gentling her along, slowly stripping every last stitch of clothing from her delectable body, stroking the warm silk of her skin, making her ready, eager for him, open and moist and willing for him, making her cry out for him as every cell in his body cried out for her, made a certain, seemingly uncontrollable part of his anatomy stand to eager attention.

Clearing his throat sharply, he reached for their cases and humped them up the polished oak stairs. Only when he was more or less sure his voice would emerge naturally did he toss over his shoulder, 'Come and pick a room out for yourself, Allie. And while you're freshening up I'll make supper. Bill—' he plucked the name randomly out of the air '—said we'd find plenty in the larder and fridge to keep us going.'

He wanted to be open and up-front with her, and truly hated this subterfuge, but he had no option but to blur the edges of the truth if he were to achieve his objective.

'How many rooms are there? It's much larger than I expected. "Holiday cottage" conjured up a two-up two-down in a patch of grass.'

The heels of her shoes beat a very feminine tattoo on the polished treads, and she sounded fluttery and strangely breathless. Surely the stairs weren't that steep! Put it down to the relief of knowing he wasn't about to renege on their bargain and suggest they shared a room, he told himself drily. He wasn't stupid enough to suggest any such thing, not at this early stage. But, of course, she didn't know that.

In the wide, panelled corridor at the head of the stairs he waited for her to catch up and told her lightly, 'It used to be a farmhouse. It was almost derelict when—' What the heck had he called his mythical old schoolfriend? Damn—he'd forgotten! To be a successful liar one needed a good memory. Normally he had the best, but in this instance it had failed him abysmally. 'When my friend bought it,' he finished, his voice shortening with self-irritation.

'There are three bedrooms,' he added more equably, and pushed open the nearest door, the one to the room his kid sister, Chloe, used when she could tear herself away from her student friends. 'You can choose, of course, but this one has its own bathroom, and you might prefer not to share the main one with me.'

He was pleased with the reasonable tone he'd managed to achieve when he'd made what he considered to be that faultless, considerate statement, and the strange look on her face puzzled him. There was a slight frown between her glorious blue eyes and her shapely head was tilted, as if she was thinking hard.

'You obviously know the house well. Do you stay here often?'

'Not as often as I'd like.' He didn't want her asking too many questions about his relationship with the owner of the property but he fielded that one with ease. It was the truth, after all. Later, when she wanted their marriage to be a real and lasting one, they'd be here more often. He could make it his base, delegate more, travel to London only when he wanted to—taking her with him, of course—and keep the Mayfair house on for when they needed it. This place, his country home, would be perfect for the babies they were going to make...

Holy cow! The thought of making babies with her

made a red mist form in front of his eyes! So cool it, he muttered to his over-active imagination, and his voice was weirdly hoarse as he queried, 'Well? Would you like to see the other bedrooms?'

Allie's eyes widened, found his and clung. Suddenly, stupidly, she couldn't look away from those black-fringed dark golden depths. He'd been reasonable, perfectly reasonable, but there'd been something about his voice, an intimate huskiness, that made her feel weak and very, very feminine.

Something was happening. She knew it was; she could feel it. Something—she didn't know what— was responsible for the thickening air that cocooned them, alternately humming softly then prickling sharply, like smooth hands that reached wickedly beneath the thin barrier of her clothing and soothed her skin, then pricked it into skittering life, made her sharply aware, not wanting it, yet craving...

She tore her eyes away from the mesmeric lights in those hooded golden ones and squawked, 'No. Not at all. This room—yes. Looks fine.' And she almost fell over her feet in her haste to cross the threshold, angry with herself for her ridiculously callow behaviour.

Thankfully, Jethro simply carried her case to the flouncy foot of the bed, said, 'See you later, then,' and left the room, closing the door behind him. Allie plopped down on the frilled, flower-patterned counterpane and swore at herself.

She didn't know what was happening to her, why she suddenly seemed incapable of thinking straight, why she acted—and felt—like an all-fired idiot! Squawking, falling over herself, imagining that some vital spark of sexual tension was thrumming in the air between them.

Twisting the thin metal band round on her finger— could it *really* be brass?—she had the manic urge to tug it off and fling it in a corner of the room. She huffed out her breath on a sharp little groan.

What the hell was wrong with her? She had asked him to marry her, hadn't she? Offered him what amounted to her life savings. He needed the money and she needed this sham of a marriage in order to give Laura the keys to Studley and tell her, It's all yours, Mum. For as long as you want it, to do with as you will.

She and Jethro had made a bargain, and so far he was sticking to his side of it. Using his friend's holiday home for a pretence of a honeymoon was a pain, but it did make sense—as he had pointed out. And he'd done the gentlemanly thing and suggested she use the only bedroom with an *en suite* bathroom to avoid the embarrassment of them accidentally bumping into each other in the shower.

So why was she getting her knickers in a twist?

No good reason. No reason at all! True, a week ago he'd been hanging around, chatting her up, no doubt fancying a fling—nothing serious, no commitments. But her offer had put a damper on his hopes for a little light fooling around in the soft summer evenings because the cash was far more important to him. Which was exactly what she had banked on.

So stop thinking about it. Stop imagining something that isn't there, she grumbled at herself.

Stiffening her spine, she stood up and deliberately took stock of her surroundings to shut him out of her mind. The pretty room looked as if it had been designed for a female. The fabrics were patterned with fully blown roses, lovely soft shades of dusky pink and heavy cream, with the pink shade echoed by the carpet and the cream by the plaster panels enclosed by exposed silvery oak beams. What furniture there was was antique pine, lovingly cared for, and the adjoining bathroom was a delight—small, but containing everything she could wish for.

His old schoolfriend must be an extremely generous man to allow them free run of his lovely home, she decided, beginning to unpack the few things she'd brought with her from the selection of slop-around-in old casuals she kept for use when she was visiting Laura.

She would ask him about his friend, she thought, as she put a pair of blue jeans and a cotton shirt out on the bed to change into. Ask what he did for a living, if he was married, had a young daughter, perhaps, whose room she was using. It would be something to talk about during what would probably turn out to be the long, dragging hours of their rural isolation.

After stripping off the blue silk suit, she sluiced her face and brushed her teeth. She'd shower later, directly after supper, and have an early night—cut down the time they actually had to spend with each

other as much as she could. In the meantime, she
thought as she buttoned the cotton shirt and secured
the slithery length of her hair into her nape with an
old ribbon, she would revert to her normal self: cool,
contained, distant.

She opened the bedroom door and went to find him.

She was back in control.

And nothing was going to change that. Ever!

CHAPTER SEVEN

SHE strode out of her room, her head high, her eyes narrowed, her jaw determined—and walked into the warm, shocking vitality of Jethro's magnificent all-male body.

The breath whooshed out of her lungs as his steadying arms immediately enfolded her, and with it went all those tough resolutions to revert to normal, to remain cool, controlled and distant.

Impossible to fight the tumultuous sensations that engulfed her as her suddenly and wickedly sensitised body absorbed the heat of his, the burning imprint of the hard wall of his chest against her tight, peaking breasts, the potent jut of his pelvis, the strength of those long thighs that were melded to her own.

And somehow her arms had gone around him, too, her hands splayed against his broad back. He had obviously changed into the soft white T-shirt while his body was still wet from the shower, because it clung damply to him, and when she moved her fingers, stroking, she could feel the tautness of his muscles over hard bone, the moist heat of his skin. Her head lifted, her lips parting, tingling, eager. Her mind had gone hazy and the only thing she could remember was the way his mouth had taken hers twenty-four hours ago. She wanted that again. Craved it with a desperation that had come out of nowhere, engulfing her with a tidal wave of need.

Kiss me.

She almost said the words out loud, and was so relieved she hadn't that she actually felt sick when he said, 'Steady on. Where's the fire?' and disengaged their arms, their coupled bodies, and told her lightly, 'I was on my way down to make supper. Come and keep me company. You can lay the table and open the wine.' His smile was kind, in a big-brotherly way, so perhaps he hadn't noticed her immediate and crazy response. But whether he had or hadn't, she felt deeply mortified.

She knew how she'd felt: abandoned and—she had to face it—wanton. His for the taking, or as good as. And that was utterly, totally humiliating.

Hadn't she spent the whole of her adult life ignoring her sexuality with no trouble at all? Surely she wasn't going to get into difficulties around Jethro Feckless Cole?

He was already clattering down the oak staircase, oblivious to the tumult he'd left behind, ready for his supper. The brief interlude that had robbed her of her now tenuous composure already forgotten.

A man who had his priorities right, she decided acidly, following, but slowly. Filling his stomach with food was more important than filling his arms with her shamefully willing body. The light-minded sexual interest he'd shown before she'd proposed this marriage had been easily forgotten because he wanted the money far more than he had ever wanted her!

For which she should be profoundly grateful, she snorted at herself. Not peeved, for pity's sake!

She turned and headed back to her room, and presented herself in the kitchen five minutes later. She'd made out a cheque to him. The figure would have emptied her bank account but it was worth it, because it was payment for the right to install Laura at Studley and because it reinforced the fact that their being here together was nothing more than a business arrangement.

Silently, holding her breath, she padded over the terracotta tiles and placed the cheque on one end of the polished oak refectory table. But he heard her—must have done—because he turned from the cooker and instructed lightly, 'Open a bottle of wine, would you, Allie? You'll find the rack in the larder.'

The wooden spoon he held in one hand swung idly towards a door between a massive pine dresser and a cavernous inglenook fireplace, and then he turned back to the meal he was making, stirring a pan which gently emitted a wreath of garlicky, tomatoey steam.

Allie wasn't going to argue with him. She'd meant to leave the room as quietly as she'd entered it, take herself for a long walk, because she wanted to get herself straightened out after the rush of lust she'd fallen prey to a scant ten minutes ago.

But somehow he'd been aware of her silent presence. So, she wouldn't get awkward about it, she'd stay and eat with him, and that way she could at least prove to herself that she was back in control of herself again and had won the battle with her wretched hormones.

The wine rack was enormous, and fully stocked. Allie felt distinctly uncomfortable as she selected a bottle of red. She didn't know a lot about vintages but the label looked expensive.

'We can't keep using your friend's food and drink,' she stated briskly as she walked back into the kitchen where he was feeding pasta into a pan of boiling water. 'Are there any shops nearby? I could replace what we've used and stock up with our own stuff.' Mentally applauding herself for the achievement of a coolly restrained tone, she added crisply, 'Your cheque's on the table. I would imagine you'd like to pay it into your account as soon as possible.'

There. She couldn't have said anything more calculated to force the business side of their relationship home if she'd tried. So if he'd noticed the way she'd clung, and stroked, and sort of—wriggled when they'd collided earlier he would have no option but to put it down to shock at being winded. She couldn't bear him to think she—well, fancied him.

Because she didn't. Well, not really. Not at *all*!

She started to hunt down the bottle-opener and Jethro said, 'The village is five miles away and the single shop doesn't offer anything more exotic than fish fingers and oven chips.' He watched her open drawers, her lovely face devoid of any expression. Not too long ago she had looked at him with drowning eyes, her luscious lips parted just asking to be kissed, her body pressed against his and making sensational little wiggling movements.

Moving away from her had been the hardest thing he'd ever had to do. He'd wanted to take what she probably hadn't realised she'd put on offer so badly he'd hurt all over. But he'd made his decision. Making love to her could wait. It would have to.

He wanted to earn her trust, her respect; he wanted her to fall in love with him and share his certainty about their future together before he took her to bed. He wanted her to be as sure as he was.

He ought to be wearing a halo, he told himself drily and said aloud, 'And banking the cheque can wait.' Until hell froze over. He wouldn't touch a penny of her money. Then he started to dish up their meal, and added, 'Bob won't mind our helping ourselves.'

She stopped fiddling with the bottle and the opener and withered him with a disdainful stare. Too late, he knew that his words, his lazy, throw-away tone, must have made him sound like the world's worst sponger, and that was no way to earn her respect!

But she said, making him sure that falling in love with her had put his brain permanently to sleep, 'You said it was Bill. The last time you spoke of your friend you called him Bill.'

Smothering a groan, he conjured up a smile coupled it with a minimal shrug, took the bottle of wine from her hands and drew the cork. 'William. Robert. He always hated both his given names,' he invented. 'And he never could decide which of the diminutives he preferred and so answers to either.'

It sounded fairly reasonable, she supposed, especially as his explanation had been delivered so smoothly. At least it had eased away the sudden suspicion that his 'friend' was nothing more than a figment of his imagination, that he had somehow discovered that the owners were absent and had decided to make free with a temporarily empty property.

She didn't want to think badly of him, to believe he was a sneaky cheat, going through life taking what he could get. It was very important to her, although she didn't quite know why. Nevertheless, watching him pour the wine, she pressed, 'What's Bill-Bob's surname?'

He didn't blame her for being suspicious. He seized his senior PA's name—he wouldn't forget that!—and gave it to her. 'Abbot.'

God! But he hated this stupid, devious game! For a moment he was sorely tempted to come clean, tell it as it was. But if he did she would wonder why, not needing her money, he had agreed to a marriage that sailed under the flag of convenience. And she would come up with the right answers and run a mile, because she sure as hell didn't want what he wanted—a real and loving marriage.

Not yet. But she would. And as soon as she did he would tell her the truth and hope she would forgive him for the deception, understand why it had been necessary.

'Shall we eat?' he suggested, and was ready for her inevitable 'Tell me about him' as she sat at the table and lifted her fork.

'What do you want to know?' He took a healthy gulp of wine. Curiosity was endemic in the female of the species; she would want to know every last detail of the fictional Bill-Bob's life! He would stick to the truth, describe himself. No more fairy tales, because he now knew for a fact that he wasn't any good at making things up and remembering what he'd said.

'Everything,' she said, deciding that it would fill what could otherwise be a conversational vacuum. Hearing about someone she'd never met, and probably never would, would be infinitely preferable to an uncomfortable silence or venturing into the realms of the personal.

'You got it,' he conceded. He'd been expecting that. Besides, it would save time on lengthy explanations later, when he came clean about who he was. Because when that time came it would mean she had fallen in love as deeply and permanently as he had, and talking wouldn't be on his agenda! He would simply refer her back to the conversation they were about to have, and—

Hastily he emptied his wine glass, and tore his eyes from the way the tip of her tongue came out to capture a speck of savoury sauce from the corner of her mouth. He applied himself to his neglected meal and gave her his own potted biography.

'He's my age. We attended the same prep and public schools, and, later, the LSE.'

So that explained the clipped, cultured accent, she decided, sipping her wine. He'd had a good education, so why had he ended up, at thirty-four, trying to earn a living cleaning windows? Some time in the future, before their final parting, she would ask him. She gave her ruptured attention back to what he was saying. She was supposed to be interested in his altruistic friend, not speculating about *him*!

'While he was at the LSE he began playing the stock markets in a modest way. He anticipated the '87 crash by a couple of months and sold his holdings while prices were sky-high, turning a modest outlay into a modest fortune—under a million. After that he began buying up failing businesses, turning them around and selling them on. Today he has an empire that covers most of the globe, and he has to be amongst the wealthiest men in the country.'

'Bully for him,' Allie said, almost dismissively. 'But what about his family? His parents, wife, children?'

His eyes hooded, Jethro poured more wine for them both. Clearly she wasn't wildly impressed by stories of fabulous wealth. The eyes of most of the women he knew would have been glittering with at best interested speculation and at worst naked avarice. But Allie, his Allie, was more interested in the human side of the man, and that reinforced his already rock-solid opinion that she was the only woman for him.

And now he was going to tell her things about his past life that he'd never shared with anyone else. She wouldn't know it, of course; she thought he was talking about his fictional friend. But, all the same, the relief of opening his heart to her was sweet. And right.

'My—' He bit the word back. He had to remember he was not supposed to be talking about himself. 'His parents lived in what I suppose you could call a minor stately home. They lived above their means and spent very little time with their son. Before he went to the local prep school the only time he left the nursery was to take a walk in the grounds with his nanny.'

'Oh, the poor little boy!' Allie interjected softly. Her eyes were misty. 'He must have been so lonely.'

So, as well as the sensual side of her nature she was at pains to hide behind that cool façade, she had a soft and tender heart. His own heart swelled with love, and he had to force himself to stay in his chair and not leap up and snatch her wonderful body into his arms, take those soft lips with his and kiss her until they were both breathless and then come back for more.

'Not a bit of it.' He denied her tender-hearted statement. He was keeping himself on a very tight rein here, and his voice sounded rough around the edges. Decidedly unsympathetic. 'His nanny, Nanny Briggs, gave him everything he needed, taught him to be independent, taught him right from wrong. She was firm, but she was fair, and she gave him far more mothering than the beautiful woman who barely noticed his existence because she was too busy having a good time, looking for—and getting—male admiration,' he explained, setting the record straight.

Her deep blue eyes thoughtful, she asked, 'You met his mother? You certainly seem to know a lot about her.'

'A couple of times,' he replied laconically. And that was as near the truth as dammit was to swearing. Vague and rare memories of a graceful form, beautifully dressed, expensively perfumed, a lilting laugh. No love.

Before she could probe any deeper on his out-of-school relationship with his 'friend' he added, 'He was twelve and away at school when his sister Chloe was born. A month after that his mother disappeared altogether—he found out later that she'd done a bunk with a Greek tycoon, and that Chloe was, in fact, only his half-sister. There was a divorce, and his father—always a remote man—withdrew completely into himself. When Bill was home on school vacations he noticed that his father totally ignored Chloe's existence. Which isn't too surprising when you consider that his wife had dumped her child on him and taken off with someone who could spend serious money on her.'

'It wasn't the baby's fault!' Allie disputed hotly. Poor children. How awful to have parents who didn't love them. And how lucky she was to have such a close bond with her own mother!

'No, it wasn't Chloe's fault,' Jethro agreed, smiling at her vehemence. 'To give the old man his due, he did keep Nanny Briggs on to care for Chloe, even though at that time he was heavily in debt—although no one was aware of it. Later, when he began to amass a fortune, Bill could have helped. But it was only when the old man died that the extent of his debts became known.' He struggled to keep the ach-

ing regret out of his voice, shared the remainder of
the wine between them and continued levelly.

'The family home was sold to cover the debts—
neither Bill nor Chloe had any fond memories of the
place—and he sent Chloe, who was fourteen at that
time, to a good boarding school, and bought this place
for them to use during the holiday times—a more
teenage-friendly place than his house in Mayfair.
Though for the last couple of years she's been more
inclined to spend her vacations with a bunch of her
student friends. She's almost through a course in interior design and seems to be doing well. For a time,
after leaving school, she went haywire, got in with a
group of seedy drop-outs. He had one hell of a
time—' And wasn't that the truth! He'd been worried
out of his mind. 'Getting her to see she was on the
way to ruining her life.'

'It will be her room I'm using now,' Allie mused,
twisting the stem of her wine glass between her fingers. 'I hope she won't mind. Bedrooms are such personal places. Is she OK now?' It was strange, but
she'd become so involved in their absent host's story.
She felt as if she knew the man, that there was a weird
kind of empathy here. She shook her head to get rid
of that kind of airy-fairy nonsense, and, smiling
softly, Jethro reassured her.

'Yes, she's fine. Fortunately he talked some sense
into his sister's head before she got in too deep. She's
working hard and playing hard, and most of the time
lives within the allowance he makes her. He could
keep her in idle luxury for the rest of her life, but he

insists she makes it under her own steam. Mind you...' he stood up and stacked their empty plates '...on the few occasions when she's overspent she can wheedle more funds out of him. She can twist him round her little finger! And as to your other question, she really won't mind your using her room. Chloe's one of the most giving people I know.'

He carried the plates and dishes they'd used over to the sink, rinsed them and put them in the dishwasher, and Allie thought with a stab of shock, He's in love with his friend's sister! The very real fondness in his tone when he spoke of her was unmistakable, and he hadn't bothered to hide the way his impressively tough yet attractive features softened with deep affection when he mentioned her name.

To her horror, she recognised the hot, hard lump in her gut as jealousy, and told herself not to be such an all-fired fool. They had a business arrangement. His private life was nothing to do with her.

Her suddenly clouded eyes watched him as he dried his hands, unwillingly skimming those wide shoulders, the narrow waist and long, denim-encased legs. Her breath caught in her throat. So much potential.

Potential for what?

She wasn't going to answer that. And when he smiled at her and asked, 'Coffee, Allie?' she nodded, looking away, because she couldn't bear to be on the receiving end of something so charged with sexual chemistry when it didn't mean a damn thing. She forced herself to think of something else.

Had falling in love with his best friend's sister

made him realise that his feckless lifestyle didn't make him good husband material? She made herself consider objectively. Was that why he'd tried to pull himself up by his bootstraps and start that window-cleaning business? Why he'd grabbed her offer of a substantial sum of money in return for marriage so that he would have something to offer his Chloe?

A year on and she'd be qualified and he would be free. Did he intend to use the money he'd earned to stake her in her own business?

It seemed perfectly and horribly logical. Allie discounted his earlier attempts to date her with no trouble at all. He was the dishiest man she'd ever laid eyes on and he had that indefinable aura of mastery that women seemed to go for. He probably had a string of meaningless affairs behind him and felt that embarking on another was no big deal. His real emotions would be kept on hold until he could go to the woman he loved without empty hands.

So why should that bother her? They weren't really man and wife, not in the true sense of the words. That had never been their intention. So why did she feel rejected, spurned? And why did the warm summer night suddenly seem so bleak and cold?

CHAPTER EIGHT

IT WAS going to be another glorious summer day. Allie had woken early, in a sober mood.

She had made a fool of herself last night, though thankfully Jethro would not have guessed the reason behind her sudden, tight-lipped statement that she'd changed her mind about that coffee, the way she'd swept out of the room giving him a brusque good-night.

He would have put her ill-mannered departure down to boredom with his company, or, worse, an arrogant belief that he, the humble window-cleaner, didn't merit normal politeness.

That made her squirm beneath the light covers. But at least he couldn't have guessed that her behaviour had been a knee-jerk reaction to the humiliation of feeling like a hurt, rejected wife! That would have been utterly intolerable!

Thrusting her long legs out of bed, she headed for the shower, pulling the roomy T-shirt that passed as nightwear over her head as she went.

She really did have to get herself sorted, stop feeling and behaving like a mixed-up wimp. She stood under the shower and waited for the needles of hot water to ease the kinks from her body and the knots from her brain.

Jethro didn't want her and she didn't want him—except, of course, for what they could get out of each other. So her dog-in-the-manger attitude when his affection—love?—for his friend's sister had hit her like a Stone Age cudgel just had to be down to the stress of the day.

Marrying Jethro had been deceitful, whichever way you looked at it—getting Studley for Laura under false pretences, deceiving Laura herself. But it had been done for her mother's future happiness, and she didn't care about getting the better of Fabian because he deserved it. In any case, he was no longer around to know what she'd done, or lose any sleep over it because just for once he'd been bested.

There was no need for her to feel guilty. Really there wasn't. Feeling guilty only led to feeing stressed out. And feeling that led to imagining she wanted Jethro to kiss her again, imagining—

Enough of that, she told herself acerbically. Quite enough. You have a year of this fake marriage to get through, so start as you mean to go on.

Pleasant, polite, but distant. Acceptably distant. And she would start by making breakfast and meaningless remarks about the weather.

Sorted. She felt better. Dressed in a pair of workman-like navy cotton trousers, topped by a sleeveless white shirt, she pushed her feet into canvas mules and left her hair loose to dry naturally.

But the kitchen clock told her it was barely seven. There was no sign of Jethro so she wouldn't start making breakfast yet. For all she knew he could favour lying in bed until noon.

She knew nothing about him, and intended to keep it that way.

'Hungry?' He walked into the kitchen via the garden door, making her practically jump out of her skin. At least she put the way her heart was doing an Irish jig down to being startled.

She blinked at him, then turned away quickly and began to fill the kettle at the sink, fumbling. Did he have to look so vibrantly male? Did he always have that aura of dangerous sexuality? Did he make every woman he came into contact with lose her backbone, lose her marbles?

The kettle overflowed, and his elegantly made, strong-fingered hand took it from her, turned off the tap. He was so close, that big hard body not touching hers, but almost. Wearing frayed denim cut-offs and a sleeveless black vest he was dynamite, his skin tanned, roughened by dark body hair. Every inch of him exuded highly potent masculinity and she could feel the heat of him, smell the clean male scent of him, reach out a hand and touch him. If she wanted to.

Her skin burned, catching fire from his. Something twisted low down inside her and she felt dizzy. She closed her eyes to shut him out and told him, 'I was going to make breakfast but didn't know if you were up.' And she wondered if that was her voice, or if a chicken had wandered in and someone was strangling it.

'One of these days you will,' he answered enigmatically. Amusement, warmth and sensuality laced his voice, but she wasn't going to ask what he meant by that remark and shuffled her feet sideways, putting very necessary space between them.

'I'll fix breakfast,' he told her. 'Why don't you explore the rest of the house, make yourself at home? I'll give you a shout when it's ready.'

At home—as if! Allie grabbed the smoothly proffered get-out with much more speed than dignity, pushed open one of the doors off the hall, closed it behind her and leaned back against the polished oak, putting her fingers to her suddenly throbbing temples, sucking in a long, shuddering breath.

She was going to have to stop fooling herself, pretending that her catastrophic reactions to him were down to stress and nothing else, kidding herself into believing that she could retain her cool composure, her indifference around him.

The unpalatable truth of the matter was that he turned her on. He was the only man who had ever made her so aware of her femininity that she didn't know what to do with herself.

Facing it and uncomfortably acknowledging it was one thing; deciding what to do about it was another. She was stuck with him and she was going to have to tough it out, at least for the duration of their fake honeymoon. Back in London, in her own spartan surroundings, involving herself one hundred per cent in her work, hopefully doing a shoot abroad, she would be able to cope, see him only when absolutely necessary for appearances' sake, put him out of her mind.

And she could do just that right now, she told herself. Stop thinking about him. Think of something else instead. This room, for instance. A long room, running the length of the house, panelled in oak with an enormous inglenook. In the winter-time there would be blazing logs to throw flickering warm lights against the walls. And apart from the faded chintz-covered twin sofas the furniture was all Elizabethan antique, obviously chosen to fit the age of the house, creating a timeless ambience.

Did her wealthy absent host fill his life with the acquisition of beautiful things because there was nothing else? She ran her fingers slowly over the glassy surface of a long Tudor sideboard and sighed. Somehow, strangely, she felt mentally tuned in to the man who had grown up without his parents' love.

Which wasn't as ridiculous at it sounded. True, until she was fifteen she'd had an idyllic childhood. Two gentle, loving parents, a deep bonding. As a family unit they'd been complete, her parents involving her in their lives, treating her as a respected equal.

She could remember painstakingly checking her father's proofs for him, discussing plots for future books, tossing out ideas which he always took seriously, could remember her mother asking her advice on the next stage of development in the garden she was creating.

So close, the three of them. So her father's death, and the manner of it, had made her defensive, made her throw herself into her work, made her hoard money as if nothing else mattered.

The door opened silently and Jethro announced, 'Ready when you are. Shall we eat outside? It's a beautiful morning.'

Absorbed in her thoughts, Allie questioned thoughtfully, 'Is Mr Abbot married?' and turned to face him, steeling herself against the now inevitable impact of him.

For a moment his eyes were blank, as if he didn't understand her question. And then they hardened, the gold taking on an arctic chill that Allie would have thought impossible if she weren't seeing the transformation for herself.

His mouth tightened and his face went hard. 'Why do you want to know? Or is that a stupid question? Natural female curiosity about the marital status of any male between nineteen and ninety who also happens to be a multimillionaire, I take it.'

He felt as if he'd been plunged into a deep-freeze. Icy cold inside and out. He'd been targeted by enough gold-diggers in his life to be able to recognise the species at a glance. He would have staked his life on Allie not being one of them.

But why else would she have asked that question?

His eyes skimmed her features, as if to find the answer there. Thick lashes veiled the deep blue eyes and a wash of colour flared on her delicate cheekbones. The colour of shame? Because he'd seen through her artless question, right into her mercenary little soul?

He felt ill with regret. If he answered in the nega-
tive and she started to simper, and asked him if he
would introduce her to his friend some time in the
future, he would walk away from this fake marriage
right here and now and leave all his hopes where this
woman was concerned to go bury themselves.

'What an unpleasant cynic you are!' She raised her
eyes at last and they fastened on his with contempt.
She pushed long silky hair back from her face with
an angry gesture and snapped at him, 'If you really
want to know, I was thinking about what you told me
about him—feeling sorry for him, wondering if the
man who apparently has everything has managed to
find someone to love. Love can't come easily to
someone who never knew it during the early, important years of his life.'

It was said with a contemptuous vehemence that
made him hate himself for lumping her in with the
others of her sex who were only interested in the size
of a man's bank balance, not caring who he was, or
what he was, what went on inside his heart and mind.

'I'm sorry.' He was, drainingly so. But it wasn't
enough. She was still bitingly angry and would have
swept past him, out of the room, but he put a hand
on her shoulder and felt her go very still. 'I overre-
acted,' he said gently. And, brother, wasn't that the
truth! One innocent question had had him verbally
firing from the hip! 'Bill's had his fair share of
women-on-the-make, trying to sweet talk their way
into his life and his pocket. For a time he got so he
didn't trust any female under fifty.' Beneath his hand

he could feel the tension in her muscles, and without conscious thought he placed his other hand on the opposite shoulder and gently, rhythmically, began to massage out the knots. 'But you'll be happy to know that he recently married the great and only love of his life.'

He felt her relax, the slender bones and warm flesh melting beneath his hands. He moved closer, just close enough to feel the sweet heat of her body. Any closer and he wouldn't be able to hack it. Already his self-control was leaking away faster than water through a sieve.

'I'm glad,' she breathed, then swallowed hard as his fingers slipped from her shoulders and gently caressed the bare flesh of her upper arms. She shuddered convulsively. Somehow she had to fight the sweetly sharp sensation that began deep down inside her and spread its heady torment to every part of her body.

Her flesh tingled, as if her veins ran with vintage champagne, and, trance-like, she spread her hands against his chest and weakly wished she hadn't, didn't know why she had, because she could feel the tautness of his muscles beneath her palms, feel the tiny tremors that told her he was as sexually aroused as she.

Which was madness. He might want a meaningless coupling, but she didn't. She couldn't open herself to the hurt that would follow. He loved Chloe Abbot; she had seen it in his face, heard it in his voice. Having sex with the woman who had bought a year of his life would be nothing more than a pleasurable way to scratch an irritating itch as far as he was concerned. But as for her—

Her brain shut down on the natural progression of that thought. She wouldn't give the unwelcome revelation head room, and panicked, her hands bunching into fists, pushing him away.

'Allie—' His deep voice shook as his hands dropped to his sides. She could see the glitter of hot desire in his golden eyes and pulled in a sharp, anguished breath. If she weren't careful she would go to him, back to his arms, give him what he wanted, take what she wanted. He was too much to handle. The temptation was greater than her diminishing reserves of self-restraint.

A mew of distress came from low in her throat and she closed her eyes in mute de-energising capitulation. If he touched her she wouldn't be able to fight it, and then she would be doing what she had always vowed she wouldn't: giving herself, her whole self, to a man and suffering the pain of the inevitable consequences, when lust turned to indifference and parting.

'I want you, Allie. And you can deny it until you're blue in the face, but the need's mutual. I want to make this marriage a real one, but you have my word that I won't push it until you admit you want that, too. Now, shall we eat?'

Confusion made her head spin. He'd talked about wanting her, making their marriage a real one, in a voice so devoid of emotion he might have been reading a shopping list. Then calmly suggested they have breakfast!

She had never felt less like eating in her life!

'That wasn't part of the agreement,' she said through her teeth, anger running through her because he'd picked up the message her treacherous body had transmitted and was using it to his own advantage, so confident of getting what he wanted he hadn't felt the need to dress up his statement with even the smallest inflexion of emotion!

'Eating?'

His lazy smile infuriated her. 'You know damn well I didn't mean that! Don't tell me you've forgotten the agreement we made—we've been married less than twenty-four hours and already you've given me advance notice that you're doing everything you can to break it.'

'Not everything, sweetheart. I haven't even begun to try.' Amusement softened his voice, sent shivers down her spine. 'I only have to come near you and something cataclysmic happens. But I've promised you I won't push it, that I'll wait until you're ready to admit it, face up to what you want.' His slow smile threatened to crumble her bones. 'We'll put the whole thing on the back burner and get to that coffee before it's stone-cold. I know I need it, even if you don't.'

He opened the door and stood aside for her to exit, and after a moment's hesitation she did, her head spinning. Putting the troubled subject on one side, as he'd so laconically suggested, was out of the question.

She was going to have to restate the ground rules again, loud and clear.

But how to do it effectively when he'd made it perfectly clear that he knew darn well how he could make her respond to his daunting sexuality without even trying, humiliating her so completely that her brain had dried up to the size and consistency of a shrivelled walnut?

It wasn't until she'd followed him outside to where he'd elected they should eat breakfast—a teak table set beneath the shade of an ancient pear tree—that the answer came to her.

She pulled out a chair and sat, watching him narrowly. He'd wrapped a padded cosy around the cafetiére and the coffee was still hot and aromatic. She accepted the cup he passed her and stated, 'We have an agreement. You've already been paid for your part in it, so I expect you to keep to the letter of it, not pocket the money and then decide you can do as you please.'

On one level she was proud of her clipped tone, the restatement of how she viewed their relationship—such as it was. On another she felt the unease of emptiness, the feeling that she was throwing away something of importance, something that could enrich her life.

She looked at the strong black coffee she needed so badly and knew she wouldn't be able to swallow a single mouthful. Her throat was too tight, painfully constricted. But there was one more thing to be said.

'You want to have sex to spice up the coming

twelve months. Forget it.' She folded her arms across her diaphram, her small chin stubborn. 'I'm not an inanimate toy for you to play with, Mr Cole. I have feelings.'

'I know you have, Mrs Cole,' he said softly. 'It's simply a question of when you're going to take them off the rein.'

Uncomfortably flustered by the honeyed softness of his voice, the mesmeric, wickedly intimate gleam of his golden eyes, his use of her married title, she compressed her lips to stop them trembling and reminded herself of the other woman. Of Chloe.

And she said harshly, 'You know nothing about me. But I think I've been around you long enough to recognise at least one genuine emotion. You're in love with your friend's sister, Chloe Abbot. As a prospective husband for his sister your friend wouldn't rate you very highly—about zero on a scale of one to ten, I'd imagine. I guess that's why you agreed to go through a marriage ceremony with me. The money. In a year's time you won't be empty handed. You could even use the bulk of it to help her start up in business, go in as her partner. Fine. But don't look to me to provide you with sex while you're waiting.'

CHAPTER NINE

SILENTLY Jethro cursed himself. His plan hadn't included putting his cards on the table this soon. He'd probably blown his chances. His only excuse was that the relief of realising that she wasn't one of the sisterhood of gold-diggers he had momentarily believed she might be had addled his brain.

Add to that his compelling physical reaction to her—her tell-tale trembling response to his earlier light caresses when he'd massaged the knots of tension from her shoulders—and his self-discipline, his will-power, had been kicked into touch.

So he'd blown it, made his intentions known far too soon. And *she'd* got this weird idea in her head concerning himself and Chloe!

For a guy who was reputed to have one of the keenest business brains on the planet he was making one hell of a mess of wooing his wife!

His wife.

Hunger for her clawed at him until the need to reach for her, crush her body to his, kiss her until she darn well *had* to admit that she felt far more than the indifference she feigned so badly was imperative. Then he'd take her to bed, make love to her until she understood that there was an incandescent beauty to the act of sex that could lead to other things. Like love. And trust.

The physical alchemy between them was earth-shattering. She was doing her damnedest to deny it but he could recognise a woman's sexual response and knew he could easily make her admit it. Heat gathered inside him. He could take her in his arms and make her lose herself, forget whatever it was that made her lock her emotions away in a cage.

But she looked so uptight, her arms wrapped around her slender body, the dappled sunlight slanting between the heavy leaf canopy making her look like a creature of the air, insubstantial as the morning mist. Her coffee was untouched and there was a haunted look in her deep blue eyes that told him she would do anything to be able to walk away. It touched him deeply.

He loved her, for pity's sake! And love for her, and caring for her, won the day. There was no way he was going to put the cart before the horse, make her admit that she wanted him physically before she was ready to trust her future happiness to him. Love came first; it had to. And trust.

There was no going back, so he had to find a way to limit the damage he'd done, and then go forward. He told her gently, 'You're barking up the wrong tree if you think I'm in love with Chloe. I've always looked on her as a kid sister, and that's the gospel truth.'

Her eyes flicked in his direction. Disbelieving? Suspicious? He had earned her mistrust and he was going to have to deal with it, say something more positive. Nevertheless, there was an up side to her misconceptions about Chloe's place in his affections.

She had instinctively tuned in to his love for his sister. Chloe was all the family he had. His father was dead and their mother hadn't been seen since she'd left shortly after Chloe's birth. He'd worried over the little minx when she'd appeared intent on throwing herself off the rails, lectured her, cajoled her, rejoiced with her when she'd finally got herself together and started to make something of her life. And Allie had picked up the vibes, which meant she was beginning to read him, get interested in him as a person in his own right and not merely a means to an end.

So that in itself was a definite plus. All he had to do was find the patience to wait. He moved her now cold coffee, poured orange juice from the jug and pushed the glass towards her with the tip of his finger.

She gave a small start, as if the gesture had been threatening, and his heart clenched painfully. He hated to think she saw him as a danger. He said soothingly, 'Chloe's a lovely lady—about your age, at a guess. Talented, sassy—a touch too much so at times—and pretty. But believe me, I have no designs whatsoever on her virtue, and as for marriage, that's completely out of the question. And Allie...' His voice lowered sinfully. 'I prefer blondes. With eyes the colour of sapphires, overlaid with violet, tall and graceful, delicate, yet perfectly formed—' He noted the faint flush of colour creep over her skin and held back.

She'd got the message; he was sure of that. He wouldn't push it. Besides, there was no going back on what he'd so misguidedly said earlier, so he had another misconception to put right.

His heart was thumping around, fit to burst itself, but his voice was level, not too light but not heavy either, as he explained, 'I meant what I said about wanting our marriage to be a real one. A lasting one. I didn't say that as a ploy to have my wicked way with you—though that would come into it. I meant for ever, till death do us part. I meant something lasting and worth having. Children, the whole bit.'

The question *Why?* sprang to her lips. She bit it back. She didn't want to hear him try to persuade her that he'd fallen in love with her. Not if it wasn't true. Did she want it to be true?

She couldn't answer that; she really couldn't. And the only other reason she could come up with for his stated wish to make this marriage real was her earning capabilities. Did he believe he was onto a good thing, seeing her as a meal ticket—no need for him to bother to go out cleaning windows for a crust?

Somehow, she couldn't believe that, either. Perhaps it had something to do with the sincerity in his voice when he'd denied having any romantic interest in Chloe, talked about making their marriage something worth having, mentioned children, but one way or another she was beginning to trust him.

The orange juice relieved the sudden dryness of her mouth, enabled her to regroup her defences, to state flatly, 'I don't want marriage. You knew that when we entered this agreement.'

It was time to back off, let what he'd said permeate her mind, gain a foothold, put down roots and bear fruit. He gave her a soft smile, a small, seemingly insouciant shrug. 'Sure I did. But you might come round to the idea, given time. You've got a year to think it over, maybe change your mind. So why don't we drop the subject, enjoy the rest of the day?' He felt the coffee pot, made a grimace of distaste. 'I'll make fresh; this is stone-cold. Eat something.'

He gestured vaguely at the croissants, the dish of fresh fruit, and headed for the kitchen. He was sweating, his heart pumping. The effort to keep everything low key, appear laid-back to the point of near idiocy had been purgatory when all he'd wanted to do was take her in his arms and kiss her, peel away every scrap of clothing from her willing body and devour every delectable inch of her with his eyes, his hands, his mouth...

He groaned and put the kettle on.

'Hungry?'

'Ravenous!' Allie responded with the wide smile that lit up her whole face, gave it a beauty that was almost out of this world. Jethro looked away before the sheer radiance of her could damage his hands-off policy, slipped the lightweight haversack—empty now of the fruit and bottled water they'd taken with them—down from his shoulders, and pushed open the French windows.

He looked back at her because he couldn't help himself. She'd caught the sun. There was a band of light freckles across the bridge of her nose, a warm flush to her skin, a dewing of sweat above her deliciously curved upper lip. They'd spent most of that day, the first of their so-called honeymoon, exploring the surrounding countryside, and her energy and enthusiasm had been boundless as they tramped fields and woodlands. Exertion and the fresh air showed in the way she looked now—sun-soaked, sleepy, a button missing from the sleeveless white shirt that had collected mossy smudges from the woods.

He ached to trace the track of those tiny freckles with his mouth, taste her sweat, run his hands through the wild tangle of her hair, strip away her clothes and his, soap her agile, graceful body under a cooling shower until her sleepy eyes glittered with desire.

Instead, obliquely giving her one of the reasons he'd fallen so heavily and permanently in love with her, he said, 'You're not obsessed by your appearance, are you, Allie? Considering the way you earn your living, I find that remarkable, and very refreshing. You've got a twig in your hair.' He reached out a hand and plucked it away. Touching the shimmering blonde rumpled mass of silkiness made his fingers tremble.

Allie gave an involuntary gasp, and in case he wondered why the touch of his fingers in her hair should make her drag air into her lungs as if she were drowning she turned it into a yawn and covered it with the tips of her fingers. She made herself relax, telling him truthfully, 'I'll put on the glam for the catwalk and cameras, otherwise I'm not interested.' She wrinkled her nose. 'What you see is what you get.'

If only! he thought savagely. He tossed the twig clear of the stone paving slabs of the terrace and ushered her in through the French windows. Keeping his physical distance, behaving himself, acting like a big brother had been harder than he'd thought. A damn sight harder. But somehow, throughout the long, hot summer day, he'd managed it.

'This must be his study,' Allie exclaimed, taking an immediate and vocal interest in the small room, examining the book-lined walls, the desk that held a laptop, telephone and fax machine. 'There must be hundreds of books.' She ran her fingers over some of the spines. Each and every one of them seemed to have been read, and her absent host's tastes ranged through Dylan Thomas, Proust, Dickens, and a handful of well-thumbed tomes on land management and environmental studies. 'Is he a closet farmer, or maybe a conservationist as well as a business brain?' she questioned, her voice painfully over-bright.

Yet the feeling of knowing the man who was Jethro's friend was oddly comforting, even if it did verge on the weird. Her compassion for his lack of parental love, the tastes they appeared to share, and deliberately putting the spotlight on him, talking about him, put Jethro and the effect he had on her momentarily in the shadows.

'I rarely socialise,' she said, noting a P.D. James she hadn't yet read, deciding to borrow it and retire to her room with it as soon as they'd eaten. Getting involved in the plot would take her mind off what was happening to her, the way he heightened her senses until the tension made her want to scream. 'Like your friend, I find books are great companions. And I suppose my love of the countryside, and my concern for what's happening to it, is down to Laura's influence and my years at Studley.'

She had the humiliating feeling that she sounded like a pathetic idiot, but she had started on this and somehow she couldn't stop. She babbled breathlessly, 'I guess he must feel at home in the open spaces, otherwise he wouldn't keep this place on, now that his sister's got a life of her own.'

'How nice of you to take such a warm interest in the man,' Jethro said stiltedly. Then mentally berated himself for putting himself in the downright farcical position of being jealous of himself! He drew in a deep breath. He wished he hadn't started out on this charade, but the wish was futile. He had to run with it until the time was right because he'd given himself no other option. And that time wasn't now.

If he were to confess that he was their absent host she wouldn't believe him, would think he was insane.

'As far as I know, he has every intention of settling here more or less permanently. It's a good place to raise a family. And you're right, of course. He is interested in conservation. We walked over a small fraction of his land today.'

He knew his voice sounded wooden, but he couldn't lighten up. He had the hateful feeling that he was getting nowhere with her. She was far more interested in the fictional Bill Abbot than she was in the flesh and blood reality. Because the flesh and blood man she'd married, the penniless window-cleaner, didn't warrant so much as a passing thought?

She'd turned her back on him, her long hair swinging forward to hide her face, but not before he'd glimpsed the heightened colour of her skin, the down-flick of the thick crescent of lashes that effectively hid her expressive eyes. And she'd reached for the silver-framed photograph of his sister, seemingly intent on committing the pretty features, the cloud of dark hair, the obstinate chin, to memory.

'That's Chloe,' he said tonelessly, almost dismissively. He needed out, needed space. He'd mired himself down in deception and had to work out how best to extricate himself before he said or did something that would ruin any hope of winning her trust, let alone her love. A project that seemed pretty damn hopeless at this moment. 'I suggest we both freshen up, then fix something for supper.'

He walked out of the room because he couldn't stand being close to her, and yet not close to her at all. He had to plan some kind of viable strategy. Around her, he couldn't think straight.

Expelling a soft breath, Allie replaced the portrait on the shelf. Chloe was extremely pretty but, unlike the other times when he'd spoken of his friend's sister, Jethro's voice hadn't held a smidgen of warmth. Did that mean that what he'd said was true, that he wasn't remotely interested, romantically, in Chloe

Abbot? Or did it simply mean that he was miffed with her, Allie?

Because she'd waffled on about his friend, the stuff they appeared to have in common? And when he'd told her that his friend owned vast tracts of the surrounding countryside he'd sounded—well, almost defeated, and that didn't sit right. Although he might be short on worldly goods he'd always come over as being at ease with himself, assured, confident. As if he could have the world at his feet if only he could stir himself to be bothered.

Her brows drawn together, she walked up to her room, stripped off and stood under the shower. Did he feel inferior to that other man, the brilliant achiever? It was more than likely, considering the gulf that now yawned between the men who had been boys together at school. Should she tell him what she believed, that worldly possessions didn't mean a thing so long as a person had integrity?

Perhaps not, she decided, pulling on clean white briefs. He would think she was being patronising, and besides, it was safer to keep their relationship as impersonal as possible.

And, come to think of it, he had spoken at length on the subject of the owner of this house, but he'd never said anything about himself, his family, where he'd lived and what he'd done before moving in with his grandmother.

So if privacy was what he wanted, that was fine by her. Non-involvement was safer.

Deciding against a bra—it had been a hot day and

didn't seem to be getting much cooler this evening—she pulled on a soft cotton T-shirt and a pair of skimpy shorts. She wouldn't say anything that might make him think she wanted to get personal. And she couldn't explain why she'd babbled on about his wonderful, successful friend either, apparently rubbing his nose in his own failure.

When he'd first suggested their outing she hadn't wanted to go, her head still buzzing with all that stuff he'd said about wanting their marriage to be a real one, the feeling she'd had of being tempted into something she'd always known would be wrong for her.

But every excuse to cry off she'd fabricated in her brain had seemed either lame or downright ridiculous. So she'd gone along, and she needn't have worried because he'd been the perfect platonic companion.

It had only been at the end of the long, strenuous but enjoyable day, when they'd been on the terrace and he'd taken that twig out of her hair, that, for her, everything had changed.

Such a small and simple thing. Just the touch of his fingers on her hair. And she had instantly become shimmeringly aware of everything about him. The height of him, the breadth of him, the scent of him, and most of all the sheer male presence of him. And suddenly, as excitement had fizzed through her veins and crackled down her spine, a real marriage to this man had become a temptation she could barely withstand.

Deeply aware of the sudden, urgent danger, she had

walked into the study and babbled fatuously.
Annoyed him. She'd made him feel inferior. And
she'd ended an effortlessly companionable day on a
sour note.

Perhaps that was for the best. Sour was better than
the other—the slide of his warm, intimate eyes over
her features as he'd restated his wish to make their
marriage real, to have children with her, the emotional
rack he put her on whenever he was near—

She could do without it.

So why the dragging sensation of loss?

She refused to find the answer to that, and went
down to the kitchen to make a start on supper.

CHAPTER TEN

THEY ate supper on the terrace. At least that was the general idea, but she noticed that neither of them seemed to be doing anything more than push the food around their plates.

Allie had grilled steaks and concocted a salad from the greens she'd found in the bottom of the fridge. When Jethro had brought wine to the table he'd said curtly, 'Don't worry, we'll replace every last crumb before we leave. We wouldn't want the man who has everything to miss out, would we?'

He was still angry with her, or hurt, or feeling diminished, she decided ruefully. She'd obviously come over as being considerably more interested in the man who had the lot than in the man she had married, who had nothing. Was that what he thought? Strangely, imagining what he must be feeling made her own heart ache in sympathy.

Allie longed to stop him hurting, to assure him that having nothing didn't matter, that if he wanted to he could go places, achieve anything, win back his pride in himself. Tell him that she would do her best to help him if he wanted her to.

But hadn't she already counselled herself that allowing their relationship to get more personal, closer than it need be was inherently dangerous? He had stated his intentions as far as their marriage was concerned, and he couldn't be blind enough to have failed to see how physically attracted to him she was. True, she'd done her best to hide her reactions, but she didn't think her best had been good enough.

So she said nothing—nothing remotely important. Just made uncomfortable small talk and watched twilight sink over the gardens, listened to the contented call of the doves. And she knew that whatever happened in the rest of her life she would never be able to hear the sound of doves without experiencing the wash of sadness that made her heart feel cold.

His statement, when he made it, took her by surprise. His voice was harsh, at odds with the softly warm twilit night. 'Are you always so trusting? Only seeing what's right under your nose and taking it as being the complete truth? Do you never look beneath the surface of things?'

He didn't know why he'd said it, only that he'd needed to lash out. Because although she had to be aware of the sexual chemistry between them she was uncomfortable with it, and seemed incapable of seeing him for the man he was. She was just putting up with him because she had to. All her admiration was for the shadowy figure of the man who owned this house, this land, a home in Mayfair, a private jet, worldwide business interests that had made him a millionaire many times over.

Her eyes narrowed as she watched him pour what was left in the bottle into her wine glass. She suspected that she had already drunk the lion's share. He had been remarkably abstemious, eating hardly anything at all and drinking even less.

'Tell me what you mean by that.'

She was watching him intently, as if trying to read his mind. She looked devastatingly desirable in the gentle half-light, her hair a shimmering drift of pale golden silk, her shadowed eyes holding his, her lips soft and relaxed, curving just slightly into a smile— dreamy from the wine?—her small but perfect breasts tantalisingly delineated beneath the soft cotton of her top, tormenting him.

Beneath the table his hands bunched into fists. He took a deep breath. He could hardly tell her that *he* was the man with everything, the man she clearly felt so much empathy for. Even if she believed him he didn't want to see her go through the process of re-evaluating everything, bestowing her admiration, her respect, on him because of what he'd achieved, not because of who he was inside himself.

Instead he told her, because it seemed as good a get-out as anything else, 'You've carved out a brilliant career for yourself in the face of what must be tough opposition. I would have thought you'd have gathered a modicum of caution along the way. Yet you leapt headlong into this marriage—I even had to stop you paying me before I'd signed on the dotted line, remember? And I would have thought you'd have had the common sense to insist on a pre-nuptial agreement. For all you know I could take you to the cleaners after the divorce, claim part of your future earnings.'

She recognised the trace of bitterness in his voice and reminded him quickly, 'I thought you didn't want a divorce.'

She didn't know why she'd blurted that out. Surely she wanted to forget what he'd told her this morning? Perhaps it was the wine talking? She decided it probably was when he leaned forward, resting his tanned forearms on the table-top, and concurred softly, not a sign of bitterness now, 'I don't. Believe me, sweetheart, I don't. I just thought I'd draw your attention to your lack of caution. It can be a big bad world out there.'

She gave a low gurgle of laughter and confessed, 'I'm not completely wet behind the ears! I trust you, Jethro. Would I have suggested this arrangement if I didn't?'

She'd always trusted him, she realised now, with a tingle of shock. On some deep, inexplicable level she had always known she could trust him.

'Do you? Trust me, that is?'

He leaned back in his chair, his arms folded across his chest. He was wearing a loose-fitting white shirt in a silky fine fabric, open at the neck, the sleeves rolled back. A slight breeze had sprung out of nowhere, ruffling his thick dark hair. It was too dark now to see his expression clearly, but she could feel the renewal of tension in him, tightly controlled.

She wanted to ease it away, but didn't know how. Unless she were to give in to the blind instinct that made her want to push her fingers through that soft dark hair, slip his shirt buttons from their moorings, slide her hands over his naked skin, find the flat male nipples with her mouth and skim her fingertips over his body, over the washboard flatness of his stomach, down, and lower down, until—

Heaven help her! She mentally stamped on her chaotic thoughts. She could trust him, but she sure as hell couldn't trust the way he affected her!

'Then let's work on that, shall we?' He seemed to have taken her reaffirmation of trust for granted. 'Tell me why your uncle felt the need to put that condition on your inheritance.'

Allie blinked. The nerves in her stomach were still haywire from the realisation that she wanted so badly to make love with this man. Her husband. Her stomach executed a few wild somersaults as the fact that they were man and wife took on a greater significance than the mere acquisition of Studley.

And she hadn't expected that question. She had expected— What? Something more intimate, an attempt to draw closer, a restatement of his own desire to make love to her?

She swallowed disappointment with a mouthful of wine, told herself not to be so darn stupid, then lifted her shoulders in a tiny shrug and told him, 'I never really blamed Fabian for refusing to renew the lease. Studley was his, he was getting married, and he wanted to live there. But I did resent the speed with which he tipped us out—I am only human. Then two years later his marriage broke down and Studley was empty again. I told you that. My mother was shattered when he agreed she could go back provided she slept with him whenever he felt like it. I despised and loathed him then.'

'That's understandable.'

Allie flicked him a glance from between her lashes, then turned her attention back to the wine glass she was holding, twisting the stem round and round in her fingers. How was it possible to be so aware of a man, so aware that nothing else seemed real?

'I—well, we didn't see him, or hear of him for years. We didn't want to. Then, soon after my career took off, I took part in a fashion show which was part of charitable event, with the inevitable party afterwards. Not my scene, but it went with the job. Fabian was there. I knew I couldn't be civil to him so I did my best to avoid him. When he tracked me down, I was ready for him. He started off by telling me I was the image of Laura as a young woman and supposed I was husband-hunting—was that why I'd chosen a modelling career, because I had a good chance of getting a wealthy man who wanted a decorative wife? He was sneering, looking me over with his nasty, knowing eyes. He told me I'd obviously inherited my brains from him—because my parents hadn't any—and that he presumed I wouldn't make the mistake Laura had: ruin my life by marrying a spineless wimp, someone who couldn't give me a decent lifestyle.

'By this point I was seething. I said I had no intention of marrying anyone, ever. And if he was a prime example of the male sex, I reckoned I'd made the right decision.'

She gave Jethro a rueful smile. 'Needless to say,

we didn't part on amicable terms, and the next I heard he'd died suddenly of a heart attack. I can only suppose he put that condition on my inheritance out of spite, because of what I'd said about never marrying, to show me what I'd lost by being so anti-marriage.'

Profound silence.

Allie shifted in her seat. Her skin was crawling with heat. She was thankful for the near darkness because he wouldn't be able to see how uncomfortable his silence made her feel.

'I don't feel ashamed of getting the better of him!' she defended hotly, when his silence became too much to bear.

She felt ridiculous when he leaned back, activated a switch on the wall that illuminated the terrace area with subdued lighting, and stated, 'I'm not suggesting you should be. I'm a partner in it, after all. A willing partner.'

The honeyed darkness of his tone sent shivers down her spine, her brain taking up the words 'willing' and 'partner' elaborating on them, translating 'partner' into 'mate', and 'mate' into 'husband'. Which was what he was. And that put thoughts she'd tried so hard to oust straight back into her head, cementing them there.

Unwittingly, her fingers gave the glass she held another violent twist, spraying drops of dark red wine on the white-painted cast-iron tabletop. Clumsily she tried to wipe them away with the tips of her fingers, but he caught her hand, held it, and she wished to heaven he hadn't because her uncontrollable fingers twined tightly around his, her body trembling at the contact of warm skin, hard bone. And the pulse-point at the base of her throat was beating so frantically he simply had to see it and know what he was doing to her.

But if he noticed how the simple handclasp had affected her he didn't show it. His voice was light, almost indifferent, as he suggested, 'Perhaps you should tell me why you made that decision. Not to marry. Ever.'

He parodied her earlier related vehemence as he said the last word, and Allie withdrew her hand as if the contact scorched her, pulling together all her reasons, wondering if he was mocking her.

Perhaps if she spelled them out he'd understand why she'd made the decision to live her life alone. More importantly, going over them would convince her of their validity.

Around him, she needed convincing all over again.

She took her time in answering, and he leaned back in his chair, his eyes shadowed, enigmatic.

'I had you down as a spunky character. Don't tell me you're afraid of love, of real emotion?' he taunted softly.

A giant fist closed around her heart. He *was* mocking her. Her reasons were sound, based on common sense. They were!

'Not afraid. Just sensible,' she contradicted coolly. 'I don't want to end up like my mother, or Fran. They fell in love, for what it's worth, and both ended up being deserted—in different ways and for different reasons, but deserted nonetheless. I saw what it did to both of them. Fran grew bitter and joyless, and my mother was simply—' she shrugged, spreading her hands in a helpless gesture '—lost, with nothing to live for. Years ago I made the decision not to entrust my dreams, or my personal happiness, into the safe-keeping of a man. And time and time again I've been proved right. I've seen too many of my friends and colleagues leap starry-eyed into marriage, only to see them, six months later, walking down the stony road to the divorce courts.

'Love, lust, whatever you want to call it, is just a word to describe the urge the human race has to re-produce itself. While it lasts it makes you vulnerable, open to hurt, makes you dependent. When it's over it leaves you empty.'

'Ah, a cynic,' he slid in smoothly when she paused for breath.

She narrowed her eyes at him. 'No, a pragmatist.'

He expelled a sigh, so faint she wouldn't have heard it if she hadn't been so tuned in to everything about him. 'You know I want you, and if you could bring yourself to admit it, the feeling's mutual. Sexual desire. You can't hide the way your flesh trembles with excitement when I'm just that little bit too close to you, the way you catch fire when I touch you.'

As if to demonstrate his effortless sexual mastery, he reached over the table, ran his hands lightly over hers and on, over the tingling skin of her forearms, until he reached her elbows. Allie's breath caught in her throat at his touch. She knew she should pull away, but, crazily, didn't want to.

His fingers tightened as he got to his feet, still holding her, moving to her side and easing her upwards, close against his powerful body.

They were barely touching, his hands resting lightly on either side of her narrow waist now, but she couldn't breathe, her lungs locked with a trembling expectancy. She lifted her face to his and met the glitter of his lowered golden eyes. She parted her lips as the trapped air shivered from her chest. She knew he would kiss her, and this time she would allow it not, as before, just for the benefit of an audience, but because *she* wanted it, craved it with an urgency that made her gasp and instinctively move closer. And now their bodies were touching, breast to thigh. The heat of him made her tremble, reduced her bones to the consistency of melted honey.

As his hands moved beneath the soft cloth of her T-shirt she arched her body, her arms clinging to him, because without his support she knew she couldn't stand. Her breasts were aching for the touch of his hands and she moaned softly, desire flaming through her as she looped her arms around his neck, her fingers twisting in the soft hair at his nape, her voice thick and heavy as she whispered, 'Touch me!'

But his hands moved away, found hers and brought them down between them before lifting them to his mouth. He grazed a light kiss across her knuckles.

'Call it the instinct to reproduce, if you like, or

sexual chemistry. Whatever, it's not a bad beginning. But there's more to it than that for me.'

His cool, measured tones flayed her. She felt cold, and lost. Terrifyingly lost. She didn't want to hear what he was saying as his eyes homed in on hers with undisguised bleakness. 'I'm in love with you. I love you. I care for you and want to go on caring for you for as long as we both shall live. How's that for starters? And, you never know, you might grow to love me if you gave it half a chance. But you don't subscribe to the view that the world is well lost for the sake of love. You won't risk emotion because you might get hurt. You might not like it, but you can't stop your body wanting mine. But you won't let yourself admit it could go a hell of a lot deeper and further than an itch to be scratched. You won't show that much vulnerability because you might be betrayed.'

He took a pace away from her, his dark shadow looming over her, and somehow he seemed even bigger and stronger, more daunting than before. Her breath shivered in her lungs. Every word he'd said had been like a knife-thrust to her heart. And it shouldn't be like that because she was right, wasn't she? He was asking her to love him and she couldn't. He was asking her to risk all the things she feared most. Hurt and disillusionment. She wouldn't.

'Go to bed,' he instructed. His voice was level but she could hear the anger beneath the surface. 'Lie in your safe, celibate bed and ask yourself if you know what you're missing. Though I doubt if your sterile heart will supply the answer, because you're a coward, Alissa.'

CHAPTER ELEVEN

COWARD.

He'd fired the word like a bullet into her brain and it lodged there, long after he'd swung on his heel and walked back into the darkened house.

Everything inside her hotly repudiated the insult. She paced the terrace angrily, her arms wrapped tightly around her body. How dared he accuse her of cowardice? How dared he?

Hadn't she been the strong one, holding her mother together after her father had thrown in the towel and taken his own life all those years ago? Hadn't she embarked on a modelling career, even though she'd hated it, as the best way of earning money quickly— the money she needed if she were to settle Laura in a country home of her own, give her back her lost security, some of her lost happiness?

It had taken her years of hard graft, posing, smiling for the cameras, always pretending to be something she wasn't, before she'd hit the big time. But she'd stuck at it. And when Fabian had, as it were, thrown down the gauntlet, she'd picked it up without a qualm and lied her head off to his solicitor.

That had taken courage. Proposing to Jethro had taken courage! So how could he accuse her—?

Her feet stilled, her stomach tightening. He'd been

133

talking about something entirely different, she acknowledged at last. Her ability to take charge of her own life, rely on herself, was not in doubt. He'd been accusing her of not being brave enough to rely on him. On his love.

Weakly, she sank back on the chair she'd been using earlier, picked up her half-full wine glass and drained the contents.

Was she brave enough to accept his love, believe in it, open her mind to the possibility of returning it?

She didn't know.

An hour earlier she had known. Had been quite definite about the lone road she intended to walk in life. The safe road. And now she was questioning it!

The question opened like a flower inside her, slowly admitting answers that were certainties. She rested her head against the back of the chair and let it happen, let the warmth grow, fizzing through her veins, the answers beginning to come thick and fast.

No other man had ever affected her the way he did.

No other man had ever reached inside her heart to make her instinctively trust him, care about what happened to him.

If their marriage ended the way she had planned it should, and he disappeared from her life, she wouldn't be able to bear it.

She wasn't going to let that happen. She knew now that she *couldn't* let it happen. He was already her husband. She was going to make him her mate. The fact that he had nothing, apart from the cheque she had given him, didn't mean a thing.

Jethro Cole had enormous potential. He wore an aura of strength and purpose, though he probably didn't know it. Together they could tap into it; together they could achieve anything!

She stood up, her spine erect, a soft smile teasing the corners of her mouth as she walked into the house. As of tonight, their marriage was going to be a real one—something worthwhile, something lasting.

She had the courage.

Jethro stared out of the master bedroom window, but it was dark and he couldn't see a damned thing except his own reflection.

He swung away from the gaunt, brooding-eyed image impatiently and pulled his shirt over his head. He might as well shower and turn in. Hanging around, trying to second guess what was going on in her mind, would do nothing but give him a pain in the head.

So much for giving her time to get to know him, to make himself so much a part of her life that she couldn't contemplate a future without him, he thought on a spurt of savage self-disgust. So much for his carefully laid plans. He'd kicked them out of shape so many times there was nothing now that could be salvaged.

Trouble was, around Allie his brain stopped functioning and his heart took over. And after what he'd said tonight there was no going back, no pretending it hadn't happened. He'd laid himself open to her. Accept his love, or reject it. But she wasn't willing to open her heart and soul to him. And he wasn't willing to take her body, even though he knew he could have done, without that much deeper commitment.

A commitment she couldn't give because he hadn't given her time.

Muttering a string of oaths, he strode down the silent corridor to the bathroom. She was probably tucked up in bed, he decided rawly, planning her escape route. Probably deeply ashamed of her sexual response to a man she couldn't love, and mortified, too, because what she'd offered had been rejected.

Hell! Why hadn't he taken what had been on offer? She'd wanted sex with him and he could have given her sex. Good sex. Good enough to build on? So why, in the name of great balls of fire, did he have to have principles!

A hot shower did nothing for his state of mind, the cold one that followed even less. Tension was knotting up the muscles of his neck; the sheer frustration of knowing his bull-headed tactics had probably alienated the only woman he would ever love was making his temples throb.

Sleep was definitely out of the question. He knotted a towel loosely around his hips. If he'd had the Jaguar he would have burned up a hundred miles or so to release his tension, returning in time for breakfast and some sort of apology for his behaviour.

But the beat-up old van—no way! He'd just have to tough out the night—dress, pick up a flashlight and walk until dawn.

His jaw set, he stalked out of the bathroom. How the hell could he have been so bloody arrogant? He'd as good as commanded her to fall in love with him, called her a coward if she couldn't! He wouldn't blame her if she tried to get him certified!

His bedroom was in darkness. He was sure he'd left the lights on. Had all the bulbs blown? Hardly likely. Probably a fuse. He moved to the wall switch, but before his fingers connected Allie said, 'What took so long?'

The soft rustle of cotton sheets came from the huge double bed and he wondered if she could hear his heart beating. He could. It sounded like thunder in his ears.

'Allie?' He sounded as if he had the croup. Badly.

There was a breath of laughter in her voice as she murmured in the darkness, 'Who else were you expecting?'

His eyes were adjusting to the lack of light. He could just make out the shape of the bed, the piled pillows. He walked over to her, hardly daring to breathe now.

No questions, because this was the most important moment of his life. What happened now, what was said, would affect both their futures—his and hers. He so desperately wanted that future to run together. So far he'd made a pig's ear of their relationship. It was down to her. He'd keep his big mouth shut and hope she'd make a better fist of this than he had done.

He could control his vocal cords but he couldn't control his thoughts. Earlier she'd been fully aroused, his for the taking, and he despised himself now for his deliberate arrogance in demonstrating how easily he could make her want him.

So was she still burning with frustrated need? Was that why she had come to his bed? To make sure he finished what he'd started? And would that be enough? Could he take that crumb and hope to build something beautiful, strong and enduring?

Reaching out to flick on the bedside light, he noted, almost distractedly, that his hand was trembling. He needed to see her properly, to look into her beautiful eyes and discover what was going on in her mind.

The soft light caressed her, darkened the huge pools of her eyes to purple. His throat tightened. Her glorious hair was spread in silky golden tendrils over the pillows she'd piled up behind her, and she was clutching the hem of the sheet under her chin.

He waited. Her eyes moved slowly—lovingly?— over his near-naked frame, sweeping languorously across the width of his shoulders, his chest, following the rough haze of dark body hair to where it disappeared beneath the towel around the jutting bones of his pelvis.

The breath tightened in his lungs and still he waited. Her naked shoulders gleamed like fine ivory above the apricot-coloured percale sheet. He swallowed around the hard lump of rock that had formed in his throat. He ached to touch her, but his need to know what had brought her to his bed was greater.

He closed his eyes briefly and muffled a groan, and she told him huskily, 'I thought about what you said, and when I stopped calling you all the nasty names I could think of I decided you were right. It's past time I stopped being afraid of having emotions.'

Her perfect breasts were rising and falling rapidly beneath the light covering which did nothing to hide the tight, hard peaks. She seemed to be having difficulty with her breathing, and when she laved her bottom lip with the tip of her tongue a great shudder racked its way through the entire length of his body.

And still he waited, forbidding himself to ask questions, to ask for more than she was willing to tell him.

'So I'll risk it,' she told him on a note of rising agitation. Her eyes skidded away from his, long lashes swept down to hide them, and she sucked on a corner of her mouth. 'I'm making a mess of this.' Her brows drew together in a frown. 'What I'm trying to do is tell you I agree with your suggestion that we make this marriage a real one.' She pulled in a sharp huff of breath, then lobbed him a look that was almost ferocious. 'You're not making this easy! Can't you say something? Or join me?'

He noted the bubble of exasperation at the back of her voice and reined back the impulse to climb straight in there with her. He had to know. Had she decided she wanted a lifetime with him, or merely thought they might as well have some fun while they waited for the year of their marriage to pass? If she'd opted for the latter it would tear him to pieces.

'Why?' he questioned tightly, his body going very still. So much depended on the way she answered him.

She made a sound that was halfway between a choke and a sob. 'Ask a stupid question! Why do you think?'

'I'm not talking about getting into bed with you,' he said rawly—and God only knew how he was holding back. 'But why change your mind about trusting your future happiness to me? We *are* talking about long-term future, I take it?'

She nodded in silent acknowledgement of that final, tight-lipped question, her head drooping forlornly. She couldn't have made a bigger mess of this scene if she'd tried. Then she heard him repeat his earlier query, but more gently this time, as if he knew how her newly found courage was slipping away from her. 'Why?'

'Because—' Her voice faltered. Suddenly she didn't know how to find the words to tell him how she felt, but the prospect of losing this man before he had really been hers made her push on staunchly. 'If love means wanting you until my whole body is burning for the touch of yours, or the thought of any harm coming to you sends me into a blind panic, or the prospect of saying goodbye to you and never seeing you again terrifies me, then I guess I can say I love you.' Her fingers were pleating the hem of the sheet, her knuckles gleaming palely beneath the tan of her skin.

He stood so still, his beautifully proportioned body tense, his golden eyes hooded, broodingly intent on hers, and she was afraid she'd made the biggest mistake of her life.

The memory of how he'd rejected her when she'd implored him to touch her flooded back, shaming her. And now she'd put herself in his bed and he wasn't interested. Did *he* have to be the one who made all the advances? Did he find women who did the offering an instant turn-off?

Had he been lying when he'd said he loved her?

A whimper of distress escaped her. She'd tried to hold it back but hadn't been able to. He moved then, as if the small sound had broken the trance that had held him immobile. The towel he wore was hastily stripped away, flung heedlessly into a corner of the room, as he slipped in beside her in one fluid movement.

His arms enfolded her and he buried his face in the curve of her neck, his breath warm against the petal-soft skin. 'I've been aching to hear you say that. I can't tell you how much.' His voice sounded raw in his throat. 'Say it again.'

'I love you.' Just saying the words flooded her with joy, released something inside her that made her feel intensely alive. She said it again, her voice shaking with happiness. 'I love you, Jethro.'

He propped himself up on one elbow to look deep into her eyes and his voice was rough with passion. 'I swear to you, you'll never regret it. I'll make you happy. I'll always be with you, loving you, adoring you.' His gaze swept to her parted lips. 'I've wanted you since I first saw you. You've become an obsession, filling my heart and mind. My sweet Allie—' He bent to kiss her and her willing mouth surrendered to his passion, her hands exploring his hard male body, sliding over his smooth, hot skin, matching his urgency as he pushed a hair-roughened thigh between the melting softness of hers and cupped her breasts in his hands.

He broke the kiss, saying her name raggedly, then pulled in a breath between his teeth. 'I don't normally have such a lack of finesse. But you shatter my control. You drive me wild.'

He was breathing heavily, his muscles tight with the effort of holding back, and she swallowed on a hot shaft of jealousy. Of course there had been others. He was a normal, highly potent male, and women would find him irresistible.

But that was in the past, and she wasn't interested in that, only in their future. She was his wife, and he loved her. She tangled her fingers in the thick dark softness of his hair, the urgent thrust of his manhood against the curve of her tummy making her giddy, the ache of need deep inside her impossible to bear a moment longer. But there was something he ought to know.

'You might be disappointed. I've—I've never made love before.' There, it was said. No need to feel embarrassed or faintly ridiculous. She was glad she'd waited for love. For him.

'Allie?' There was a catch in his voice. 'You're a virgin? Such a gift you bring me—second only to the gift of your love.'

He pulled her gently into his arms, and the touch of his skin on hers was fire and silk, and the touch of his hands on her woman's body was sensual, unhurried now, deeply erotic, her shudders of response making his body shake as the slow seduction of her senses had her writhing in his arms.

And when at last he took her into the wild heaven of sheer ecstasy she knew she was fused to this man for ever, body and soul.

CHAPTER TWELVE

'NOT even heaven could be this good!' Allie said as they slowly made their way from the honeysuckle-covered gazebo back to the house.

'No contest!' His fingers tightened on hers. Soon he would have to tell her who he was, but not just yet. He knew Allie's gorgeous head wouldn't be turned when she learned she'd married serious money. His sweet darling loved him for himself, not for the luxurious lifestyle he could give her, so it wasn't that that was holding him back. He simply didn't want anything of the outside world encroaching on their private paradise.

Ten perfect days. Day of making love, discovering each other, the people they really were beneath the trappings of success. Two loving people.

His heart swelled inside him and he swung her round, gathering her into his arms, kissing her with all the depth of his passion, and when she surfaced for air she was breathless, clinging to him, her eyes that lovely shade of misty amethyst that told him more plainly than any words that she wanted him.

She moulded the shape of his naked shoulders with the palms of her hands, her head tilted, her hair sun-bleached and wild where he'd tangled his fingers in the long silky strands. 'We don't really want supper, do we?' she suggested, her voice a sultry invitation. Already her body, naked beneath the cotton shirt of his she was wearing, was unbearably sensitised. She dug her bare toes into the cool green grass, stretching up to fit the apex of her thighs against the surge of his arousal that the brief shorts he was wearing did little to contain.

'Not yet awhile.' His eyes gleamed into hers as he moved against her provocatively. 'Bed calls, don't you agree, sweet wife?'

She was too far gone to answer, and curled her arms around his neck, nibbling his tanned shoulder as he swung her up and carried her back to the house. But the phone was ringing—an unprecedented event since they'd been here, an unwanted intrusion.

'You'd better take it—it's probably for your friend,' she told him as he slid her down to plant her on her feet.

'Or ignore it?' he suggested, his eyes wicked, teasing her as she shook her head. 'Well, if you insist—just don't change your mind about going to bed.'

'As if!' She lifted her hand and put two fingers briefly and tenderly across his mouth. 'Answer it, before it explodes! Give me a shout if it's my mother.' She wandered towards the kitchen, the tail of the borrowed cotton shirt brushing against her thighs. She had never been so happy in her entire life.

She took a carton of apple juice from the fridge and poured herself a glass, hanging around in case the caller *was* her mother. She'd spoken to Laura shortly after they'd arrived, to let her know they'd got here safely, that the old van hadn't fallen to pieces on the way, that the house and surroundings were idyllic.

She would have to persuade Jethro to change the wretched vehicle for something that promised more reliability. She sipped her cold drink and decided that stuff like that could wait.

When they'd set up home in her tiny flat they could discuss how he could best use the money she'd paid him. If he wanted to carry on cleaning windows, that would be fine by her. She'd have to talk to him about keeping proper books, advertising his services, getting proper insurance. But it could wait.

They had two days left before their two weeks were up and she meant to make the best of them, not start wittering on about his work prospects, how they would manage when she had to give up work when the child they both wanted was on the way.

The line of his shoulders was tense and irritable when he walked into the room. She rinsed out her empty glass and said, 'It obviously wasn't my mother. Would you like apple juice?'

He shook his head to both, but he didn't elaborate on who the caller had been. 'I'll go for something stronger.' He reached the chilled white wine from the fridge. 'Like some?'

She watched his long, lean fingers deal with the foil round the neck of the bottle, insert the corkscrew. The simple task surely didn't merit that grim look around his mouth.

'Is something wrong?' she asked. He seemed, suddenly, to have gone away from her. 'Tell me if there is.' It had to be that phone call. Could it have been the owner of the house, his old schoolfriend, asking him to leave because he needed the place himself? Was that why he was looking so impatient?

'Of course there's nothing wrong.' Nothing but Chloe's rotten timing. Determinedly, he put his sister's phone call—the ramifications of which could mean trouble—to the back of his mind. For what was left of their time here his priority was Allie.

'Why should there be?' He drew the cork, tucked two glasses in one hand and the bottle in the other. It would be their last night of being just themselves in this paradise; nothing was going to spoil it.

The real world of big deals, boardrooms, chattering faxes, business meetings on the other side of the world, his sycophantic entourage of secretaries, managers, assistants and minders would encroach soon enough. He would explain everything to her tomorrow. Tonight was for them, and only them.

He gave her the slow, intimate smile that always turned her spine to water. 'I believe, Mrs Cole, that you and I have a date with a bed.'

And so the incident was temporarily forgotten.

Very much later she stirred in his arms. He was stroking her hair. Maybe he hadn't slept. She had. His lovemaking had reached new heights of intensity; she couldn't believe anything, ever, could get better than that. She turned her head drowsily. 'What time is it?'

'So Sleeping Beauty finally wakes.' His fingers traced the line of her profile. 'Almost dawn.' The pads of his fingers rested on her mouth. 'We'll leave today, head for London.'

Allie twisted her head to look at him. In the grey pre-dawn light his features looked sombre, his eyes shadowed, unreadable.

'I thought we'd be here until the day after,' she protested. She'd made plans for their final full day here: take a picnic to the secluded lake in a fold of the thickly wooded hills, swim in the cooling waters, make love on the mossy bank...

'Afraid not, sweetheart.' He settled back against the pillows, crossing his arms behind his head. 'You need to see that solicitor to sort out your inheritance—time's moving on, remember. And I need to see someone about a business venture.'

Nothing that couldn't have waited one more day, surely? She lifted herself up on one elbow, her head tilted as she peered into his face. His eyes were firmly closed. He wasn't fooling her; she'd heard the regret in his voice because he hadn't been able to hide it, and she knew he was as reluctant as she to end this blissful rural idyll.

'What business venture?' Was he trying to set up something that would secure their future? Did he have contacts in London through the old-school network? Or was it simply an excuse?

She suspected it was the latter when he merely said off-handedly, 'Tell you all about it when it's sorted.'

He could explain now, he thought. There was time before they need get up and begin to pack. How to begin, though? Would she see the whole thing as amusing? Understand why he'd made the decision to keep the reality of his life from her? Or would she view it as plain and simple deception, stop trusting him?

But she took the problem of how best to state his case right out of his mind when she wrapped her arms around him and nestled her head against his chest. 'This place is a million times better than my poky pad, but to tell you the truth, my dear love, I don't care where we are as long as we're together.'

She was sure now that the call last evening had been from his friend, asking him to move out. During their time together she'd recognised Jethro's natural authority and knew he would be chafing inside because he was having to deprive them of the final day of their honeymoon. But he was in no position to object.

The poor darling would be feeling diminished, and she couldn't bear that. One day, though, she vowed fiercely, he would find his full potential. She found his flat male nipple with the tip of her tongue and ran the fingers of one hand down the washboard hardness of his stomach, and he gave a deep, guttural groan and turned and gathered her to him.

'That's it, then?' Jethro lifted her suitcase and carried it down to Harry's van. They were running late. He'd left her to sleep in while he'd made one or two necessary phone calls, gone round closing windows, made coffee and toast for breakfast. But she'd insisted on stripping the beds before they left, cleaning the kitchen.

'We can't leave the place in a mess. And what are we going to do about replacing everything we've used?'

His response had been non-committal to the point of indifference; she probably thought she'd married an ungrateful slob.

Now, as they left the van in the station car park, she said worriedly, 'Can you just leave it here? Won't it be towed away?'

'Save me the bother of driving it to the scrap yard,' he answered, his attempt at humour failing because they were going to miss that train and he was having to hustle her through to the ticket hall.

So she'd be thinking he was irresponsible, too. Though one of his earlier phone calls had been to Harry, to tell him where he'd find the van. He could pick it up, sell it for what he could get for it. Probably twopence-halfpenny—it wasn't worth any more!

He'd bought two first-class tickets on his credit card, and when they entered the carriage, a split second before the train moved out, she said, 'We can't stay here. It's first class.'

She looked adorable, pink and flustered, dressed in a pair of narrow-fitting white linen trousers topped by a cool lemon sleeveless cotton shirt. The band of freckles across her nose had widened. He wondered how long it would take him to count them.

He gave her a slow smile. 'Relax. I have first-class tickets.'

'Do you know how much they cost!'

'An arm and a couple of legs,' he said drily.

Great, just great! She would now think she'd married a spendthrift. She subsided into her seat and he smothered a sigh. He would spill the beans tonight.

He joined her, taking her hand, idly twisting the cheap wedding ring round on her finger. He would replace it with something more worthy of her.

'Humour me,' he said softly. 'I want nothing but the best for you. And as tonight's the last night of our official honeymoon, I'll take you out to dinner and thoroughly spoil you.'

He knew the perfect place. An exclusive hotel near Windsor, with Georgian elegance, a menu and wine list to die for, a candlelit dining room, the tables set in islands of privacy, the bridal suite boasting a four-poster bed.

Another of this morning's early phone calls had reserved the suite, and a table for two. His senior PA, James Abbot, would drive them there this evening, collect them at noon tomorrow. It would be the perfect place, the ideal setting for his explanations.

'I don't need spoiling, but dinner would be nice.' She returned the pressure of his fingers and stared out of the window thoughtfully.

If he wanted to splash out then she'd do as he said and humour him. The money she'd paid him was his, after all. But they did need to have a heart-to-heart about the need to be careful in future.

They'd made love more times than she could count and her cheeks went pink just thinking about it. But they'd never once taken precautions. Why should they when they both wanted a family? Even now she could be pregnant.

The thought of having a baby with him made her stomach clench, made her give a tiny breathy gasp, and Jethro said softly, 'What are you thinking?'

She turned to look at him, resting her head against the upholstered back of the seat. Her hair was loose again today, and it spilled down to her shoulders and framed her face with its pale gold silkiness.

'Thinking how much I love you.'

And that was so true her heart squeezed tightly beneath her breasts. He looked both charismatic and commanding, despite the fact that he'd opted to wear the cheap, poorly cut suit he'd worn for their wedding over a cut-price shirt with a collar that refused to lie flat and a tie so chewed-looking he had to have borrowed it from his grandmother's husband, Harry, or from some obliging tramp!

Her dear darling was doing his best to look smart for her benefit, packing away his usual worn denims and T-shirts. But what he wore didn't matter to her; it was the man he was that counted. She would never have believed it was possible to love someone as extravagantly as she loved him!

It took all of two minutes to show him round her tiny, spartan flat. When he carried their suitcases to the bedroom she told him, 'Sorry about the single bed. We'll have to manage on that until I can arrange to have a double delivered.' She gave him a rueful glance. 'I've never tried to make it homey, so we'll put our heads together and see how best to brighten it up.'

'Don't worry about it,' he replied uninterestedly. 'And don't bother unpacking for me; I'll see to it later.' He shot a look at his watch, dropped a light kiss on the end of her nose. 'I'd better make a move. I'll pick you up this evening at seven. Wear something special.'

'That business meeting?' she asked quickly. 'Shall I come with you?' Whatever it was he had in mind she didn't want him to jump into something iffy because he needed to provide for their future.

'No.' The shake of his dark head was very definite, his voice clipped, as if he felt she was wasting his time. 'Get an appointment with your late uncle's solicitor. If Laura's to live at Studley you'll need to get permission to have the keys before probate. If the place has been empty for some time we'll need to check that it's habitable.'

She watched him leave the flat and tried to pull her heart up from the soles of her shoes. Would the business meeting last all day, right into the evening? He'd been in such a hurry to dump her here and get away, had shown no interest whatsoever in the place that would be their home until they could afford to move to somewhere bigger.

His main interest, it appeared—apart from getting away—had been in making sure she claimed her inheritance.

Because he knew how much Laura wanted to move

back there, or because it was an extremely valuable property?

She caught that thought and stamped on it with great determination. She wouldn't think that of him. She would *not*!'

If he wasn't interested in his new home she could hardly blame him. It had little to commend it. He was preoccupied with his business meeting, and that was understandable. And hadn't he already said that he'd tell her all about it when it was finalised? He wasn't stupid—he wouldn't touch the venture if he wasn't sure it would be successful.

She trusted him implicitly.

CHAPTER THIRTEEN

THE appointment with the solicitor was fixed for two days hence. Allie scribbled the time in her diary and wondered whether to phone her mother, realised she would probably be out at work and decided to phone her agent instead. She riffled through the pad she kept on the telephone table until she found the agency's new number.

She needed to start earning again, but she would refuse anything that took her overseas. She wouldn't spend any more time away from Jethro than was absolutely necessary.

'Darling—you're just who I need!' Christa Fisher screeched. 'Absolutely heaven-sent. You're going to dig me out of a hole; I know you are!'

Allie grinned, well used to her agent's histrionics. But all that effusion hid a very sharp business brain and Allie said, 'Have you got anything for me? Fairly local—my days of travelling the world on assignments are over. I'm a married woman now.'

Anticipating Christa's shriek of delighted disbelief, Allie held the receiver away from her ear, and when she gingerly replaced it the other woman was saying, '...several possibilities. The Pure Magic cosmetic people asked for you— I told them you were resting,

155

but they're still looking. I'll get on to them right away.

'Now, that hole I was talking about. My dear, would you believe it? Marietta's let me down. She was supposed to be the star of a charity fashion parade and gala tonight. She phoned and called off this morning. The stupid cow's fallen and broken her collarbone, would you believe! What she thought she was doing, tramping some grouse moor with some titled Hooray Henry, I simply cannot imagine! I fixed Sasha Dell up as her replacement, but she simply hasn't got your style. Now, why don't we do lunch and discuss it?'

'Tonight's not—'

'Must fly!' Christa warbled. 'See you in an hour—that trendy new place—Dosser's, Covent Garden, yah?'

Wryly wrinkling her nose, Allie replaced the buzzing receiver and scribbled down the name of the lunch venue on the open pad, beneath Christa's number. True to form, her agent hadn't let her get a word in. But lunch would pass the time. She could find out what work was on offer and explain that Christa would have to stick with Sasha Dell for tonight's gala. She was having dinner with her husband, and no way would she cancel that date!

An hour gave her just enough time to pile her hair on top of her head, apply light make-up, and step into narrow indigo-blue trousers and a matching slim-line jacket. It was one of her few decent outfits, kept for when she needed to look understatedly elegant.

Jethro had told her to wear something special to-night. Her mouth softened. She'd dazzle him with the black she kept for gala appearances: figure-hugging silk with a sculptured sequinned top kept in place by the narrowest of straps. She would show him she could look a million dollars if she wanted to!

She was five minutes late when the taxi deposited her outside Dosser's. 'Trendy' was the operative word, she decided as she was shown to Christa's table.

Great quantities of chrome and smoked glass gave the restaurant a Fifties feel, with portraits of film icons of the era smouldering down from the walls and a Presley tape playing in the background.

'Sorry if I kept you waiting,' Allie apologised as she slid into her seat. 'The traffic was horrendous.'

'No worries! I've decided that this place is not my scene. I just hope there's more on the menu than hamburgers and frothy coffee.' Christa flicked her fingers at a passing waiter. 'Another G and T, and plenty of ice. And for you, darling?'

'Spring water with a twist of lemon.' Allie picked up the menu, grinned when she saw the dreaded hamburgers, slid her eyes down and found a seafood salad that sounded just right.

'But, as I was saying, this would be a good place for talent-spotting—they all seem so young! For instance, there's a dishy dolly at one of the window tables, lunching with her lover. Darling, an absolute hunk! He was called away to the phone seconds before you arrived. Can you see her? Dark hair, bright red dress?'

She rested her pointed chin on her hands, narrowing her bright hazel eyes. 'Restyle that hair, decent make-up, a really good photographer, and she could be a winner. What do you think?'

Anything to oblige! Allie had to move her chair slightly to be able to look back into the main body of the room, towards the windows. And because of the position of the other occupied tables she could only see the girl's head and shoulders.

Chloe Abbot, surely. She could clearly recall the pretty face in the silver-framed photograph, the untamed cloud of dark hair, the slightly obstinate chin, the pouting, leaf-shaped mouth. If that girl wasn't Chloe, she was her double. It would be something interesting to tell Jethro this evening. She wondered who her lover was.

'Her face has character,' she agreed, smiling, and turned back to Christa, who was downing her second gin and ordering for them both. 'The seafood salad, yah?'

'Fine,' Allie concurred, ready to talk business, explain that she wouldn't be available this evening.

But Christa asked, 'Now, tell me about this husband of yours. Thought you weren't interested. He must be quite something to have made you change your mind. So when did it happen? My God! Is that thing your ring!'

Allie's eyes flashed with temper. She didn't care if

her wedding ring looked as if it had come out of a Christmas cracker!

Fortunately for their future working relationship, Christa stemmed the cutting remarks all ready to spill off the end of Allie's tongue by gripping her wrist with a red-taloned hand. 'The hunk's back. Ain't love sweet! And, look, I do believe he's writing out a cheque—don't tell me it's for services rendered! He doesn't look as if he has to pay for it!'

Christa was outrageous. 'Keep your voice down!' Allie admonished with a giggle. No one could stay miffed with her for long. Then, twisting in her chair to find out what was so intriguing, she knew she wouldn't be smiling again. Not for a long time.

Jethro was wearing a slate-grey suit, Savile Row's finest, a million miles away from the one he'd worn to their wedding. His shirt was a crisp pale blue, his tie a sober slate and blue narrow stripe, his thick dark hair freshly barbered. His aura of power and supreme self-confidence was very evident.

She didn't really mind if he'd chosen to spend her savings on improving his packaging; if he wanted to muscle in on the business world then it was probably a good idea. But she was damned if she wanted him to pass a chunk of it over to his—whatever she was!

Because that was obviously what he was doing. She saw him re-cap his pen, slide his chequebook back into an inner pocket, push the narrow slip of paper over the table and lift his hand to slide his fingers lovingly down Chloe's adoring face.

Frozen with shock, Allie found he couldn't look

away. Everything seemed to be happening in slow motion, branding each action into her brain. When she saw the girl in red reach up to take that softly caressing hand, hold it tightly within her own, she felt sick.

Jethro had lied to her all along. He was definitely romantically involved with his rich friend's sister. She was seeing the evidence with her own wide, strained eyes, absorbing it with every tight, shallow breath she took. Which meant that—

She couldn't bear to go into that, to face what those lies of his actually meant. Not now, not here. She would think about it later, when she felt calmer. She turned her back on them both just as her seafood salad was put in front of her.

The king prawns, the scallops, the strips of smoked salmon, the coating of sauce... She clutched at the sudden searing pain in her stomach. She was going to throw up; she knew she was...

'Are you all right, darling?' Christa's concerned voice seemed to come at her in waves, from some far distant, misty place.

She mustn't make an exhibition of herself in here. She *mustn't*! If she sat here, very still, her back to the main part of the room, then Jethro wouldn't notice her. His attention was all for the vibrant young woman in red, in any case.

But another hot stab of agony gripped tight in her stomach. She said through a painfully forced smile, 'I'm fine. Just need to go to the loo. Excuse me.'

When she'd entered she'd noted a sign, garishly lit,

saying 'Dolls', and she pushed herself to her feet now and headed in that direction, keeping her back to the body of the room. Deep within the mess of her emotions she did have some pride left. Jethro mustn't see her, see her distress. When she asked him to explain himself she had to be in full control of herself.

Thankfully, she wasn't sick. She locked herself into a cubicle and rested her hot forehead against the cool aqua wall tiles.

Jethro had lied to her. Everything she'd believed to be so beautiful in their marriage was nothing but a cynical untruth.

When he'd first talked about Chloe Abbot, his wealthy friend's sister, feminine intuition had told her he was in love with the girl. Her guess that he'd married her, Allie, to get his hands on enough money to prove to his friend that he wasn't a penniless no-hoper when, after the divorce, he was free again to marry Chloe, had been horribly correct.

Not that they'd need her brother's approval, of course. But he wouldn't want to alienate a man with all that money!

And the Studley inheritance came into it. The thought hit her like a dash of icy water. Had he been, in effect, warning her of what would happen when he'd accused her of being too trusting, of not insisting on a pre-nuptial agreement because without one he could take her for all he could get, claim half she owned when they divorced? In spite of what he'd said, the marriage would end when it suited him.

She stifled a sob, her aching heart telling her it

couldn't be true, clutching at straws. How could he have made love to her with such passion, such tenderness, if he was in love with another woman?

But she'd seen the two of them with her own eyes, hadn't she? Had recognised the woman he was with, her brain reminded her cruelly. And he was a man, wasn't he? A highly sensual man. He'd certainly picked up her sexual response to him, taunted her with it. Why shouldn't he take advantage of her body while he was waiting for the deeds of Studley to fall into her hands?

She had to get a grip before she completely went to pieces, stop torturing herself with questions she couldn't answer. Straightening her wilting spine, she told herself that she'd have the whole thing out with him tonight. He was taking her to dinner, supposedly—if he could tear himself away from Chloe Abbot. With a touch of cynicism she wondered if he would wear the grotty suit he'd worn earlier or that elegant slate-grey number.

The cynicism was healthy, she decided. It helped. Helped her when she exited the cubicle. Helped when she found Chloe drying her hands under the hot air.

Rinsing her own hands, Allie watched the other woman walk to the mirrored wall and said conversationally, 'Do I know you from somewhere? Chloe Abbot, isn't it?'

Chloe had a lovely smile. She glanced back into the mirror, raised her left hand to push her cloudy dark hair back from her face. A wide gold band glinted on her wedding finger.

She's married! Allie thought with a stab of incredulity. Was Jethro poaching another man's wife? When he'd talked so affectionately of his rich friend's sister he hadn't mentioned that she was married. Or did the scene she'd witnessed back in the restaurant have a viable explanation after all? Had she been thinking terrible things about him for no just reason? Her head began to spin.

'No, I'd have remembered if we had met,' the other woman said. Again the lovely smile. 'And it's Chloe Cole, not Abbot. Not a very euphonious moniker, but I'm stuck with it.'

It took all the backbone Allie possessed to march out of the room.

Apart from all the other horrors, she had married a bigamist. There could be no other explanation!

Frowning, Chloe watched the abrupt departure of the tall, elegantly beautiful blonde. Then, shrugging slightly, she twisted the diamond of her engagement ring back into place. It kept slipping round, the stone digging into her palm. They would have to get the band made smaller.

Back at their table, Allie re-seated herself and fended off Christa's 'What the hell took you so long?' with the arch of one brow.

'Don't ask embarrassing questions, darling,' she said smoothly, then speared a prawn and followed up, 'What time do you want me for this evening's do? And where?'

She felt icily cool now. She had strength. No man would turn her into a lost wreck of a creature, or fill her with the acid of bitterness that would, in the end, ruin her life.

She had her life; she had her future. She had herself to rely on. She didn't need more.

Fran had been right, and all her own earlier instincts had been spot-on. No man could be trusted. They all betrayed you in the end.

CHAPTER FOURTEEN

EVERYTHING had gone smoothly, Allie assessed coolly. But then, any event organised by that indefatigable fundraiser Madeleine Floyd-Palmer always did.

Backstage, the usual chaos had reigned. One of the designers had thrown a tantrum, and at one point the principal co-ordinator had threatened to walk out. But, as far as their audience was concerned, the food and wine served at immaculate tables set around the ballroom and the fashion show had been perfect.

'There you go.' The dresser undid the last of the dozens of tiny silk-covered buttons that ran down the back of the fabulous wedding gown and Allie stepped out of it, was glad to.

Modelling the beautiful confection, smiling as she did her slow solo walk beneath the softly strobing lights, had put the first dent in the armour she'd assumed since she'd told Christa she would accept this assignment. The dreamy, romantic music had brought a sheen of tears to her eyes, made her think of Jethro, of what might have been.

Which was an exercise in futility, she told herself now tartly, ignoring the chatter—a lot of it bitchy— as half a dozen models got into their own clothes and endlessly fussed with their hair and make-up.

They, and the designers, were expected to mingle with the dinner-suited or bejewelled diners back in the ballroom of this prestigious hotel. Dinner over, the stage would be cleared for dancing, and they'd be mingling with the *crème de la crème*, who had paid through the nose to attend, not only to support a fashionable charity but to be seen to be doing so.

I'm turning into a cynic, she thought. But then she had every reason to, hadn't she?

As the changing room emptied she took the black silk with the daring sequinned top from a garment bag, stepped into it and pulled the zip at the back that cinched the slinky, glittery bodice to her like a second skin.

She was going to do her duty, mingle and smile. She was going to party. She'd left a note for Jethro, propped up against the telephone. 'I'm working tonight.' She hadn't added sorry, only, 'Don't wait up.'

Because she'd be late. Because she needed to delay the final confrontation for as long as possible. She had to be sure she could handle it with icy dignity. She couldn't afford to go to pieces, to let him see how badly his treachery had hit her. Her trust, her love, had been shattered. She had to keep her pride intact.

She placed the suit she'd arrived in in the empty garment bag, stepped into high-heeled black pumps and faced the mirror. Despite the expert make-up her face looked pale, her eyes too big and haunted.

Suddenly the idea of partying was out. She couldn't do it. The thought of it made every nerve in her body go tight and painful. Unwilling to change yet again, she hoisted the strap of the garment bag over her shoulder, picked up her purse and made her way to the foyer.

Pointless to delay the inevitable. The small dent occasioned by wearing that wedding dress had been successfully ironed out. She was right back in control. A few more hours wouldn't make the coming confrontation any easier. The doorman hailed her a taxi and she gave the address of her flat, but, travelling along the Embankment, she ordered tightly, 'I've changed my mind. Let me out here.'

'Are you sure?' His middle-aged face showed his concern. Possibly, she thought, because her hand was shaking as she passed him his fare. She nodded, her throat too choked to allow her to speak, and she saw him shrug fatalistically as she turned away.

She was all wired up again. How could she face Jethro, tell him what she knew about him, what she'd seen—the wedding ring on the finger of the girl who had been Chloe Abbot and was now, on her own admission, Chloe Cole—while her battered heart was raw and bleeding?

She would have to make sure she was together before she saw him. Since lunchtime today she had believed she was. But that wretched wedding gown had triggered a relapse. She had thought she'd mentally dealt with that too, but obviously she hadn't. She needed more time.

Tears sprang to her eyes blurring the view over the river. The low evening sun had dipped behind a cloud and the river looked dark and oily. Lights gleamed, throwing dancing reflections across the water.

Why couldn't she stop loving him? Why couldn't she stop hurting? He didn't merit this much of her emotion. Her mind accepted that but her stupid heart wouldn't.

The breeze from the Thames cooled her skin. She shivered, heard firm footsteps just behind her, felt a sudden rush of air, smelled exclusive aftershave, felt strong arms around her as he turned her taut body into the warmth and strength of him.

Jethro. Her knees gave way. How could she be clinging so weakly to him when she knew what he was, was fully aware of how cruelly he'd used her, how callously he'd made her love him and trust him when all the time he had betrayal on his mind?

The palms of her hands connected with the broad span of his shoulders. The fabric of his jacket felt smooth and expensive. Her shocked eyes evaluated the white dinner jacket, the black tie, his shadowed face piratical in the dying light.

She gave an ineffectual shove, her breath choking in her throat, but he cupped her chin in one hand, forcing her to look at him, swearing softly beneath his breath as he saw the tracks of tears on her pale cheeks.

'Get in the car,' he commanded tersely, retrieving her scattered belongings with one hand, the other clamped around her waist. Wildly, she thought of digging her heels into the paving slabs, telling him she wasn't going anywhere, not with him, not ever again.

But already a few passers-by were hovering, looking curious. Heaven only knew what would happen if she caused a scene.

Visions of a fracas, the police, the press, lurid details of her bigamous marriage splashed all over the sleazier tabloids flashed behind her eyes. She shuddered, giving in, allowing him to hurry her towards the waiting car.

The well-bred engine of a Rolls Royce Silver Shadow was ticking over quietly, and Jethro opened a back door and slid onto the luxurious leather upholstery beside her, telling the driver, 'The Blue Boar, James. Quick as you can.'

What was happening? What was he doing? Allie panicked, tried to scramble out before the big car picked up speed, before a police car appeared behind them, blue light flashing, sirens wailing, but Jethro's hands clamped around her narrow waist, anchoring her to the seat.

'Calm down, sweetheart. I know what you're thinking, and I know why you're thinking it. And every last bit of this mess is my fault.'

He'd gone cold all over when, at the end of a long afternoon, after he'd driven his sister to her bank to pay that cheque into her account, after his second meeting with her brand-new fiancé and his own company solicitor to thrash out the details of the partnership deal the newly engaged couple were entering into, Chloe had said, apparently apropos of nothing, 'Now I think of it, her face was familiar. She's either a top model or maybe an actress. She said she thought she knew me, but she got my name wrong. Abbot, she said. I think it was Abbot.'

When he'd prised out every last detail of that fateful meeting in the restroom at Dosser's he'd known what Allie would be thinking. He'd been cursing himself every second since.

The car had gathered speed now, and he could feel her prickly antagonism. It was reflected in her voice as she asked him, 'Where did you get the Roller? And don't tell me you went out and bought it—along with the sharp suits—out of the money I paid you. I'm not that stupid.' She turned to look at him, her pale face shadowed in the near darkness, her soft mouth pulled into a bitter line. 'And where the hell do you think you're taking me?'

'To dinner. We had a date, remember? And I know you're not stupid, sweetheart. You're adorable and deeply loved.' He took her hand, twining his fingers with hers, and almost she believed him, believed the deep, honeyed sincerity of his voice—until she remembered what an opportunist he was, using her for what he could get out of her, both financially and sexually.

She withdrew her hand, wrapped her arms around her body and he told her, his voice low and gentle and laced, unbelievably, with a thread of humour, 'I haven't stolen the Rolls, if that's what you're afraid of. I keep it to ferry foreign business visitors around London. It seems to impress. And James Abbot, the driver, is my senior PA. His discretion can be relied upon absolutely. Nevertheless, I think we should keep this conversation on ice until we reach our destination.'

In her emotional chaos she'd actually forgotten they weren't alone. The driver's ears were probably flapping. And what had he called him? James Abbot? Not Bill or Bob. Did he always forget people's names? Was the driver his wealthy friend? Oh, she didn't know what was going on!

'How did you know where I'd be?' she asked, keeping her voice as low as possible. 'I didn't leave an itinerary.'

'You did—or as good as. I found your note, saw you'd written your lunch venue beneath your agent's number, and phoned her. She told me where you'd be this evening. I waited outside, followed your cab when you left. Simple, really.'

Simple! Nothing was simple or straightforward around Jethro Cole.

She gave up trying to figure anything out, subsiding into the corner of the seat and telling herself that as soon as they reached their destination—wherever that was—she would ask the driver to explain what was happening, because she didn't trust a word Jethro said!

But the plan didn't work. How could it when, almost as soon as her feet hit the gravelled forecourt, Jethro, already out and standing on the other side of the luxurious car, tapped his hand on the roof and the Rolls drew away, purring back down the long, tree-lined driveway.

Discreet lighting displayed the gilded name of the

hotel above the Georgian portico and security lights gleamed on the immaculate paintwork of expensive motors. Some of the cars even came complete with patiently waiting uniformed chauffeurs.

So they weren't alone. They were in a public place; he hadn't brought her to some lonely, desolate spot. She had no reason to be afraid, knew she could never fear him, no matter what situation they found themselves in. He wouldn't harm her physically; the very thought of that was absurd. But he could hurt her heart, break it so easily. Already it was battered and bleeding, and it was up to her to make sure he didn't damage it even further.

'What now?' she asked tiredly across the small space between them. He was holding her garment bag and a compact leather overnight case of his own. It had been a long, traumatic day. In the space of a dozen hours she'd gone from being an ecstatically happy bride of less than two weeks to a bitter, betrayed dupe.

'I'm giving you dinner. We had a date, remember? And we're staying overnight. In the bridal suite. James will collect us tomorrow and drive us home. We have a home in Mayfair. You haven't seen it yet, but I'm sure you're going to like it.'

He spoke softy, feeding her information bit by bit, his heart twisting inside him because she looked so fragile and vulnerable. He ached to take her in his arms again, to feel her immediate response to his body, to take away her hurt. But he had to tread carefully. He knew he was on very thin ice here. And the whole damn thing was his own pig-headed, selfish fault.

Dismissing most of what he'd said, her mind fixed on the three words that terrified her so much she couldn't take anything else in.

The bridal suite.

She couldn't spend the night with him; she simply didn't dare. Her emotions would betray her. She couldn't fight the way her body needed his.

He had closed the gap between them, and his hand on the small of her back was edging her towards the three shallow steps that led to the entrance. She had to find the strength she needed to resist, to quell the treacherous voice in her mind that was asking if it mattered if she spent one last night with him, accepted the ecstasy that only he could give her.

Digging stiletto heels into fine gravel, she said forcefully, 'Stay here if you must, but I want you to call me a taxi. If you're looking for a romantic dinner for two and a night of purple passion, then call your legitimate wife! Or was lunch enough to satisfy her?'

His hand slid further round her waist, tightened. He could so easily lift her off her feet and carry her in. His mouth softened with tenderness. 'I saw our passion as being more gold than purple, sweetheart. Pure, twenty-four-carat gold! And as far as I can recollect, you're the only wife I have. Or want. It was my sister who had to be satisfied with lunch. Shall we go in? Or would you prefer to talk about it out here? Though I warn you, it's all a bit of a tangled mess, and sorting it out could take an hour or two.'

Her head was spinning. She allowed him to walk her into the muted elegance of the hotel's foyer without even thinking about it. She wanted to believe him, but how could she?

He had never mentioned the existence of a sister before. He never talked about himself. She knew as little about him now as she had done on the day she had offered to pay him for marrying her.

And she knew for a fact that his lunch companion—very close companion—was the former Chloe Abbot whose married name was Cole. Hadn't she seen the shiny gold wedding band with her own eyes?

He was devious and tricky, a smooth charmer. Right now he seemed to be charming someone who looked like the hotel manager—a very deferential hotel manager. And now a porter had taken their ill-assorted luggage. A recent school-leaver, she guessed, looking very proud of his smart uniform. And she was with Jethro, mounting the sweeping staircase towards the dreaded bridal suite.

She was only going along because she had to get at the truth, had to tell him that she wasn't some empty-headed bimbo who would swallow a lorry-load of lies provided they led to a night of out-of-this-world sex!

Nothing to do with wanting to believe him when he'd said she was the only wife he had, the only wife he wanted.

The suite was fabulous. Even her tired brain was able to register that. Sitting room, bathroom, bedroom. Furnished in the period, softly lit, with lush carpets and the decor subtly blending tones of old rose, soft sage-green and cream. Fresh roses perfumed the air and champagne was on ice.

At the sight of such opulence, the decadence of the huge four-poster bed, she crossed the room and closed the bedroom door firmly, hating the way her face seemed to be burning. Jethro was pressing something into the young porter's hand.

'We're later than I anticipated, have more to talk about, too. So we'll eat here. I've already ordered for us both.' He shrugged out of his jacket, removed his black tie, saw the way she narrowed her eyes at him and assured her, 'I can pay the bill. You won't have to spend the next two months of your life washing dishes.'

The fine white cotton of his shirt clung to his upper body; she could see the faint shadow of dark body hair, almost feel its crispness beneath the tips of her fingers. She swallowed hard. How could someone who was so bad look so mouthwateringly good?

Remembering just why she was here with him, she ground out impatiently, 'I don't give a damn how you spend the money you earned from me. Fancy hotel room, expensive suits and a hired Rolls don't impress me. What would impress me is the truth—why you lied about not being romantically involved with your friend's sister, why she's changed her name to Cole, why she's wearing a wedding ring, why you were smooching over lunch. I'm not interested in the rest of the garbage,' she flung at him. 'The house in Mayfair, the fancy car kept to impress visitors, the personal secretary—or whatever it was you said he was!'

She was pacing the floor, didn't realise she was doing it until he took her by the shoulders and turned her gently round to face him.

'Sweetheart, why don't you sit down? If you'll listen I can explain everything.' His fingers grazed her naked shoulders, and of its own accord her body began to sway into his.

So sitting down seemed like a great idea. She felt the edge of a chair at the back of her knees and sank into it, closing her eyes briefly as physical and mental exhaustion washed over her in a huge black wave. And when she forced them open again he was holding a slip of paper in his hand.

'Recognise this?'

It was the cheque she had given him shortly after their marriage. She watched him slowly tear it into tiny pieces, her fingers flying to her temples.

'I don't understand!' Not this, not anything. Offering him that money had been the only way she could persuade him to marry her.

'Of course you don't. How could you? But you will; I promise,'

His promises weren't worth the air he uttered them with, and she wasn't prepared to sit and listen to whatever make-believe he decided to tell her.

She jumped to her feet, eyes wildly scanning the room for where her purse had landed up. 'I'm out of here! If you won't call me a taxi I'll do it myself from Reception. I don't want to be here. I don't know you!'

He was quicker than she was. He reached her long before she got to the door, pinioning her arms at her sides, his eyes insistent as they held her own. 'You know everything about me.' He saw panic flare briefly in her lovely eyes, followed by the sheen of tears. Her soft lips were trembling. She was almost at the end of her tether.

Pulling in a ragged breath, he said gently, 'Think back, Allie. At the cottage, I told you everything about the owner. Everything I said was true, except his identity. I got his Christian names mixed up, and when you wanted to know his surname I gave the name of my PA because I knew I wouldn't forget that. I was telling you about myself, my darling. Chloe is my sister—half-sister, to be precise. And of course I love her—we've come through some sad, bad times together.'

Hardly daring to breathe, he carefully folded his arms around her. It was like holding a ticking time bomb. She was so wired up she could explode at any moment, or she could swing the other way, settle down and listen. At least she wasn't struggling in his arms, demanding to get away from here. But she wasn't relaxing, either.

He felt a tiny tremor ripple through her body, felt the loosening of tension in her muscles just as someone knocked on the door. Turning, he swore under his breath, saw the trolley, the white-coated waiter, and snapped, 'Not now, Mike! Bin it, and bring the order back, fresh, a bit later on. Better still, phone through first!'

'That wasn't very polite,' Allie said stiffly as the door closed behind the trolley. And she pushed herself away from him. What had she been thinking of, letting him hold her when she knew very well how being close to him made her forget everything else?

'I wasn't feeling polite. As majority shareholder in this establishment I guess I'm entitled, for once in my life, to throw my weight around. I'll apologise later—fulsomely. OK?' He smiled at her, saw the way her face tightened before she turned her back on him, and said heavily, 'I'm not shooting a line, Allie. Everything I say to you is the truth.'

She gritted her teeth to stop herself from having hysterics. Did he know what the truth was? Could she believe anything he told her? Did it all come down, in the end, to trust?

And please, God, she prayed fervently, don't let him smile at me again. Don't let him touch me because my brain cells all close down when he does!

But nobody was listening to her, because he came to stand behind her. Her hair had started to tumble down and he moved his fingers through it, releasing the pins, letting it fall down her back.

'Try to relax,' he said, and began to massage her shoulders, her neck, loosening the kinks in her taut muscles, moving the narrow sequinned straps out of the way. And Allie, betrayed by the sheer magic of his touch, by what it did to her, felt her whole body blossom for him and burst into noisy sobs.

Smothering a groan, he lifted her in his arms and carried her, clinging to him, sobbing wretchedly, to the bedroom, eased her hands from their stranglehold around his neck and laid her on the bed.

He wanted to join her, to hold her close, but he slipped the shoes off her narrow feet instead, then knelt at her side, holding her hands until her sobs became sniffles, and then he reached a tissue from the box on the bedside table and handed it to her.

She blew her nose fiercely. She hardly ever cried. She must look an unholy sight, her eyes all puffy and red and her nose swollen and pink. She hated him!

'If,' she challenged imperiously, 'you are so all-fired wealthy, with homes all over the place and half a hotel, and a Rolls, and goodness only knows what else, then why the sweet blazes were you cleaning windows, driving a wreck? Why did you agree to marry me when I mentioned the pay-off?'

'Don't forget the Jag and the private jet, and various businesses all over the world.' He grinned shamelessly at her. She looked so feisty, so adorable, even if the end of her nose was a radiant pink. He rose to his feet, sat on the bed beside her, anchored her body to the soft mattress by leaning one arm across her.

For a moment he thought she would try to wriggle away, but she didn't. She seemed scarcely to be breathing, her eyes very wide. And his own eyes clouded as he admitted, 'I lied to you about who I was because I'm a selfish bastard. I only thought about what I wanted. I wanted you to love me for myself, not my bank balance. I'd had my fair share of women who came on to me for what they thought they could get out of me. I saw you for the first time over a year ago. I'd been dragged along to a fashion show and you were the model everyone was talking about.

'I was smitten, couldn't get you out of my head. I could do nothing about it because for the next twelve months I was living out of suitcases around the world. I thought all my Christmases and birthdays had come at once when you appeared at the bottom of the ladder that day to thank me for helping Laura. I was practically struck dumb. And, to put the record straight, I was helping Harry out. He'd come down with flu and Nanny Briggs—'

'*That's* Nanny Briggs?' she asked quickly. Suddenly, somehow, it was all beginning to hang together. She'd felt so sorry for the little boy who had known nothing of parental love, remembered how Jethro had assured her that he'd had the best kind of mothering from Nanny Briggs. 'I thought she was your grandmother.'

'I know you did. And I let you think it, let you think I was on my uppers, scraping a living cleaning windows. When you explained your need to marry, offered to pay me, I jumped at it. I took you to my holiday home, told my staff to keep well out of the way, gave myself a couple of weeks' head start in the game of getting you to fall in love with me—head over heels, as deeply in love as I already was with you. Only it wasn't a game. It was deadly serious.

Because I knew you were the only woman I would ever love.

'I almost blew it a couple of times. I pushed you too fast, too far. I couldn't stop myself. I wanted you so desperately. I didn't for one moment stop to think how the truth, when it eventually came out, might affect you. That you might think I'd somehow made a fool out of you, deceived you.'

He removed his arm, no longer imprisoning her. She was free to go if she wanted to. And his voice was low, unsteady, as he told her, 'I know material possessions don't mean much to you. I know you loved me when you believed I had little more than the clothes I stood up in and a rusty old van. I'll understand if you can't love a man who lied to you, no matter how good he once thought his reasons were. I'll understand, and I'll make some sort of fist out of trying to handle it.'

He watched her thick lashes sweep down to hide her eyes. She lay very still. Was she turning everything over in her mind, deciding she couldn't love a liar?

His body went cold, his heart smothered in ice. How would he bear it if he lost her now? How could he live with the regrets, the lack of her love?

And then she raised her hand to touch his hair, raised her eyes to reveal the shimmer of tears, and her voice shook a little as she said, 'I always felt I had a strange kind of bond with your mythical wealthy friend. I remember you telling me of his early life, telling me how he couldn't love because he couldn't trust, how he never knew if people—women especially—wanted him or his money. I could always understand that. Now I know you were talking about yourself, how you felt, I can understand it even better, because I love you so much you're part of me. I couldn't trust emotions, either. I was afraid of them, afraid of being hurt, abandoned.'

'Sweetheart!' His voice was raw with passion as he took her hands and kissed every one of her fingers. 'I don't deserve you, but I'll do everything I can to try to!'

She drew his hands back to her, rested them against her breasts, her eyes wicked as she whispered, 'Start trying right now. I'll let you know how you're doing!' Her breasts were hardening, the tight sequinned fabric barely containing them; heat was pooling heavily inside her and her body went boneless for him as his fingers found the back fastening of her dress—just as the telephone rang.

His face went dark red as he reached over for the instrument, and Allie giggled, putting a hand over his. 'Politeness costs nothing, remember? And even if it did, you could afford it, apparently. You did suggest the poor man phone first, didn't you?'

His smiling mouth covered hers just briefly before he said into the receiver, 'Order's cancelled, Mike. My wife and I have everything we need.'

And then he finished what he'd started.

Hours later, Allie stretched her arms above her head languorously, revelling in the touch of Jethro's hard, hair-roughened body against the silky smoothness of her own. His dark head stirred on the pillow, the arm that was flung possessively around her tightening.

'I'm hungry,' she said. 'Absolutely starving. I haven't eaten since breakfast—and then you only gave me time to swallow one piece of toast—and I couldn't eat my lunch because I'd seen you and Chloe. You didn't tell me she was married.'

He hauled himself up against the pillows and flicked on the bedside light that made the four-poster look like a rosy cave. His darling wife looked rosy, too, flushed with lovemaking. He glanced at his watch. 'Are you always so talkative at three o'clock in the morning?'

'Probably.'

He gave her the slow smile that always made her heart flip over. 'Chloe isn't married, but I can understand why you thought she was. When she held out her hand to show me her ring all I saw was a plain gold band. It's too big for her and the stone slips down, out of sight.'

Echoes of the shock she'd had when she'd seen the two of them together, the terrible sense of betrayal and hurt came back, haunting her. She raised her knees to her chin and looked at him sideways. 'I could have met your sister, had lunch with you both. You needn't have left me the way you did.'

'I know,' he sighed. 'I made a pig's ear out of everything. Our honeymoon was coming to an end and I was going to have to tell you the truth about me. I'd planned on telling you on the last day at the cottage. Selfishly, I wanted to hang onto the magic of knowing I was loved for myself. But it was Chloe who phoned last night. She'd met this up-and-coming interior designer, Guy Fellows. They'd fallen in love and she wanted me to buy her a partnership in his one-man business. Knowing her track record, I was worried, told her I'd need to meet him first, take a look at his accounts. Hence the dive back to London. I'd planned to get the business with Chloe and her fiancé out of the way, leaving myself free to concentrate on you, bring you here, tell you everything. You'll get to meet Chloe soon enough.'

'I'd like that. And Nanny Briggs. Properly.'

'Then you forgive me?'

'Well…' She gave him a teasing smile. 'I probably would if I weren't so hungry.'

To prove her point her stomach grumbled. Jethro slid his long legs out of bed. 'I'll see what I can do.'

'There might be packets of nuts in the mini-bar,' she suggested, but he fetched one of the towelling robes from the bathroom. 'I think I can do better than that. I know where all the keys are kept. Keep sweet for me, my love.'

Sweet. She slid out of bed and went to shower, rubbing body oil into her skin. It smelt of honeysuckle and roses. She was insanely happy. How could she have lost her trust in him? And hadn't she always known that, despite appearances to the contrary, he had huge potential, could achieve anything? How hard he must have had to work to create such wealth.

Something would have to be done about that.

Ten minutes later, both clad in towelling robes, they were sitting at a small round table eating the smoked salmon, hard boiled eggs and crusty rolls Jethro had foraged for. Between sips of champagne, Allie said, 'You don't need to earn any more, do you? Or are you a workaholic?'

'Used to be.' His eyes gleamed at her. 'There didn't seem to be anything else. Now there is.' He raised his flute to her, his golden eyes glittering, the line of his mouth sensual. 'I've decided to sell off the majority of my holdings, delegate more where the ones I'll hold onto are concerned. The cottage would be the ideal place to bring up our children and I'd like to concentrate more on conservation. We'll keep the Mayfair house on, for when we feel like being in London. It will be handy for showing the children the sights—the Tower, Hampton Court, all that stuff. Of course—' he grinned at her '—selling up will make us even more disgustingly wealthy, but I guess we can handle that. What do you say?'

'I say we can handle anything, as long as we love each other,' she replied huskily, her eyes drenched with devotion as she watched him rise to his feet.

He took her hands and pulled her up. 'Do you think you could live with a broad gold band and a diamond bigger and better than anything in the Crown Jewels to replace that cheap brass thing?' he asked softly. 'I hated having to put that on your finger when I wanted to cover you with precious gems.'

'Being covered with jewels sounds a touch uncomfortable,' she dimpled at him. 'But I get your drift.'

Her fingers strayed to the narrow band of base metal. 'Call me sentimental, but I wouldn't exchange my wedding ring for all the gold in the Bank of England. However...' She smiled at him, misty-eyed. 'A diamond to go with it would be acceptable—if it makes you happy!'

Jethro swallowed the lump of sheer happiness that had lodged in his throat, and his voice was raw with passion as he told her, 'I'll never stop loving you. I love you more with every breath I take. And now...' He untied the belt of her robe. 'I believe it's my turn to be hungry.'

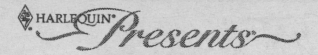

HARLEQUIN *Presents*

Legally wed...
Great in bed...
But he's never said,
"I love you"...

Wedlocked!

The bestselling miniseries from
Harlequin Presents®

Coming September
BOUGHT: ONE HUSBAND
Harlequin Presents® #2132
by Diana Hamilton

Available wherever Harlequin books are sold.

Some secrets are better left buried...

Yesterday's Scandal by

Gina WILKINS

A mysterious stranger has come to town...

Former cop Mac Cordero was going undercover one last time to
find and exact revenge on the man who fathered, then abandoned
him. All he knew was that the man's name was McBride—a name,
that is synonymous with scandal.

...and he wants her!

Responsible, reliable Sharon Henderson was drawn to the sexy-as-
sin stranger. She couldn't help falling for him hard and fast. Then
she discovered that their love was based on a lie....

YOU WON'T WANT TO MISS IT!

On sale September 2000 at your favorite retail outlet.

HARLEQUIN®
Makes any time special ™

Coming Next Month

HARLEQUIN *Presents*

THE BEST HAS JUST GOTTEN BETTER!

#2133 INNOCENT SINS Anne Mather
Eight years ago Laura Neill had innocently stolen into her stepbrother Oliver's room and discovered ecstasy in his arms. This is Laura's first visit home since. Can she face Oliver without confessing the love she still feels for him?

#2134 THE PLAYBOY'S VIRGIN Miranda Lee
Brilliant advertising tycoon Harry Wilde needed a challenge. It came in the guise of Tanya, who'd recently inherited an ailing firm. In no time at all Harry had helped her take charge—and had fallen for her. But Tanya wasn't the marrying kind—and he only ever had affairs....

#2135 SECRET SEDUCTION Susan Napier
Nina had lost her memory, but it was clear that stranger Ryan Flint recognized her. He seemed angry with Nina, and yet intent on seducing her. When their passion finally exploded, what secrets would be revealed?

#2136 MISTRESS OF THE SHEIKH Sandra Marton
Sheikh Nicholas al Rashid is hailed in his homeland as the Lion of the Desert, and Amanda has been commissioned to refurbish his already luxurious Manhattan apartment. Just why does Nick seem so intent on making Amanda his mistress?

#2137 A MOST PASSIONATE REVENGE Jacqueline Baird
When Rose meets society bachelor Xavier Valdespino again, he immediately whisks her to Spain and blackmails her into marriage. But despite their steamy love life, Rose soon discovers Xavier's true motivation: revenge!

#2138 THE BABY BOND Sharon Kendrick
Normally Angelica would have liked nothing better than to look after Rory's orphaned nephew—she adored babies. But this baby was her ex-husband's love child, and Rory was the brother-in-law who'd always held an illicit attraction for her....